HOW THE EXPERTS DO IT

How the Experts Do It

Improving your Bridge

TERENCE REESE

and

DAVID BIRD

faber and faber

LONDON · BOSTON

First published in 1985
by Faber and Faber Limited
3 Queen Square London WC1N 3AU

Filmset by Wilmaset Birkenhead Merseyside
Printed in Great Britain by
Redwood Burn Limited
Trowbridge Wiltshire

British Library Cataloguing in Publication Data

Reese, Terence
How the experts do it
1. Contract bridge
I. Title II. Bird, David, *1946–*
795.41'5   GV1282.3
ISBN 0–571–13463–7
ISBN 0–571–13464–5 Pbk

CONTENTS

PART 3   PAST THE POST

FOREWORD

Most bridge books are aimed at, and read by, one of two classes: comparatively new players who wish to improve, or a faithful group – not tournament players, as a rule – who will read almost any new book by an author they know.

David Bird and I have had in mind on this occasion the very large class who have played the same sort of average game for many years and have a vague feeling that with a little effort they could improve at least to the level of the best players in their group. This is not so much a textbook, therefore, as a stepping-stone.

Terence Reese

Part 1

THEY'RE OFF!

1

PLANNING A TRUMP CONTRACT

The arrival of dummy is always an exciting moment. The
defenders will inspect it from their point of view. Has the
opening lead worked well? Is the dummy weak or strong in
terms of the bidding? Meanwhile, as declarer, you will be hard
at work planning the play. See how you fare on this six-spade
contract. West leads a trump.

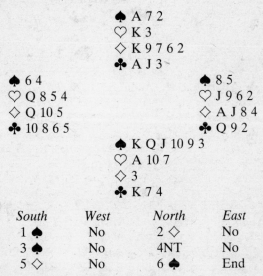

	♠ A 7 2	
	♡ K 3	
	♢ K 9 7 6 2	
	♣ A J 3	
♠ 6 4		♠ 8 5
♡ Q 8 5 4		♡ J 9 6 2
♢ Q 10 5		♢ A J 8 4
♣ 10 8 6 5		♣ Q 9 2
	♠ K Q J 10 9 3	
	♡ A 10 7	
	♢ 3	
	♣ K 7 4	

South	West	North	East
1 ♠	No	2 ♢	No
3 ♠	No	4NT	No
5 ♢	No	6 ♠	End

Look at the losers in the hand with the long trumps (South).
You have one heart loser, but that can be ruffed. In diamonds
you expect to lose one trick. In clubs you have one possible
loser, but the club finesse may succeed or you may have found
♢ A onside, allowing you to discard a club on ♢ K. So, the
contract appears to depend on one of two finesses.

Is there any other chance? Yes, you may be able to establish dummy's diamond suit for a discard. Win the trump lead in hand and lead a diamond immediately. The king loses to the ace and East returns a trump. Win in dummy and ruff a diamond high. Cross to ♡ K and ruff another diamond high. Good news! Everyone follows. Cash ♡ A and ruff a heart. Now take yet another high diamond ruff and draw the outstanding trump. You can reach the established diamond with ♣ A.

Note how important it was to play on diamonds immediately. If you had drawn a second round of trumps first, you would not have had enough entries to establish the diamond suit.

Let's look at another slam, similar in some ways to the first. How would you tackle seven hearts on this deal?

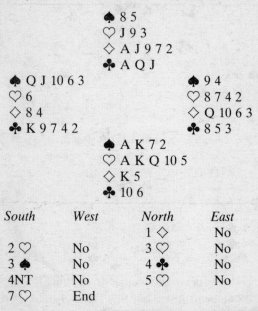

	♠ 8 5	
	♡ J 9 3	
	◇ A J 9 7 2	
	♣ A Q J	

♠ Q J 10 6 3		♠ 9 4
♡ 6		♡ 8 7 4 2
◇ 8 4		◇ Q 10 6 3
♣ K 9 7 4 2		♣ 8 5 3

	♠ A K 7 2	
	♡ A K Q 10 5	
	◇ K 5	
	♣ 10 6	

South	West	North	East
		1 ◇	No
2 ♡	No	3 ♡	No
3 ♠	No	4 ♣	No
4NT	No	5 ♡	No
7 ♡	End		

Taking a rosy view of your hand, you arrive in seven hearts. West leads ♠ Q. As always in a suit contract, your first move is to count the losers in the hand with the long trumps. You have two spade losers, but they can be ruffed with dummy's high trumps. There is also a loser in clubs. You could take the club finesse or perhaps establish a discard on dummy's diamond suit. What is the best sequence of play?

Win the spade lead, cash the other high spade and ruff a spade with ♡ 9. Now play the king and ace of diamonds and lead a third round of diamonds. East follows, so you ruff with the ace. Unfortunately West shows out. If diamonds had broken 3–3, you would have been able to draw trumps and run twelve tricks.

You will now need the club finesse to be right. Since the club suit will provide a discard in this case, there is no point in ruffing the fourth spade. You finesse ♣ Q successfully, draw trumps in four rounds and repeat the club finesse. Your second spade loser is discarded on the club ace.

Both the hands we looked at contained the three principal elements of card-play in a trump contract: *ruffing in the dummy*, *finessing*, and *establishing discards*. In the next three chapters we will take a closer look at each of these techniques.

QUIZ ON PLANNING TRUMP CONTRACTS

West	East
♠ A K 6	♠ 10 8 3
♡ A K Q 10 7 3	♡ J 9
◇ 3	◇ A Q 8 5 2
♣ 9 5 4	♣ A K J

South	West	North	East
			1 ◇
No	2 ♡	No	3 ◇
No	3 ♡	No	4 ♣
No	4 ♠	No	4NT
No	5 ♡	No	6 ♡
End			

You reach an excellent heart slam and North leads ♣ 2. Plan the play.

ANSWER TO QUIZ

There is no need to risk the club finesse at this stage. Win ♣ A
and cross to hand with ♠ A. Now take the diamond finesse – this
is slightly better than playing South for ♢ K x x or ♢ K x.
If the diamond finesse loses, there are still good chances of
establishing a long diamond for a second discard. Use ♡ J and
♡ 9 as entries for two diamond ruffs. If the diamonds break 4–3,
you can draw trumps and enter dummy with ♣ K to discard a
spade and a club on ♢ A 8. If the diamonds fail to divide, you
will take the club finesse.

2

FINESSING

Newcomers to the game find a hypnotic attraction in the finesse, imagining they are conjuring extra tricks from thin air. The expert is not so entranced. He is more concerned with arranging the play so that he can avoid taking the finesse. However, that is not always possible and it is important to know the correct way of playing the more frequent combinations. You may be familiar with these holdings:

(1) ♣ A J 9   (2) ♡ A Q 9   (3) ♢ K 10 9

♣ 7 4 3   ♡ 6 5 3   ♢ 8 6 2

On the first holding you begin with a deep finesse of ♣ 9. If this forces the queen or king, a subsequent finesse of ♣ J may succeed. You score two tricks if West started with Q 10, K 10 or K Q 10.

With (2) you will always make two tricks if West holds the king, so try the effect of a first-round finesse of the 9. This will gain a trick when West holds the J 10 and East the king.

Holding the third combination you start with a finesse of ♢ 10. If this loses to the jack or queen you will finesse ♢ 9 on the next round. It is important to realize that finessing the 9 on the second round is much superior to leading towards the king. The first play wins when West started with either the queen or jack. This is obviously more likely than finding him with just one specific card, the ace.

Declarer played well on this hand, which offered several finessing possibilities.

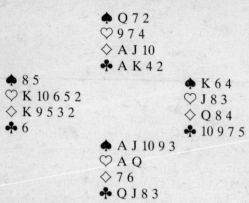

West led his singleton club against six spades. Yes, six! We said he played it well, not bid it well. Declarer won with dummy's ♣ A so that he could finesse in the trump suit. Since a low trump to the jack would leave him in hand with no satisfactory entry to repeat the finesse, he led ♠ Q from the table. East covered and declarer drew trumps in three rounds.

He now led a diamond and finessed the jack, losing to East's queen. Back came ♡ 3. Our hero put up ♡ A, refusing the heart finesse, and led a diamond to the 10. When this second diamond finesse succeeded, he was able to throw his heart loser on the diamond ace and claim the contract.

Why did declarer prefer the second diamond finesse to a heart finesse? As with the K 10 9 holding we looked at, the second diamond finesse was appreciably better than an even chance. East's diamond holding might be headed by the Q or K Q. Since a defender with K Q may play either honour, the play of the queen provides an assumption that he holds *only* the queen.

You will often initiate a finesse by leading an honour. Before doing so, always ask yourself if you can afford the honour to be covered. These are common positions:

(1) ♡ A Q 7 6 2   (2) ◇ A 10 7 5 (3) ♠ K 10 9 7 2

  ♡ J 5 3   ◇ Q J 4 2   ♠ J 6 4

With (1) you never gain by leading ♡ J, and it will cost you
a trick if West has ♡ K x or ♡ K singleton. The best play
depends on how many tricks you need from the suit. Aiming for
five tricks, you must play low to the queen, hoping to find West
with ♡ K x. To play safe for four tricks you cash ♡ A first,
gaining when East has a singleton king.

On the second holding, leading an honour from hand will cost
you a trick when West has a singleton king. Assuming entries
are plentiful, you should start with a low card to the 10. The
same principle applies on (3). Leading the jack will cost a trick if
West holds a singleton queen.

With many combinations you cash a high honour before
finessing – but which one?

(1) ♣ K Q 10 7 2 (2) ♡ A Q 9 6 5 (3) ◇ K Q 9 7

  ♣ A 9 6 5   ♡ K 7 4 2   ◇ A 10 4 2

The first holding will be familiar to you. You cash ♣ K, one
of the touching honours, guarding against ♣ J x x x in either
hand. Beware of (2), though, which is a false cousin of the
previous holding. The only 4–0 split that you can negotiate is
♡ J 10 x x with West. You should therefore play ♡ K on the
first round.

With (3) you start with ◇ K. If a fairly innocent player on
your right drops the 6 or 8, play him for the singleton. If East is
an experienced and knowledgeable player, the situation is
different. Does he rate you as the sort of mug who would be
deceived by the play of the 8 (from J 8 x x)? Here we cannot
help you.

There are some interesting combinations involving the ace,
queen and 10. Do you play these three holdings correctly?

(1) ♠ A 8 2　　(2) ◇ A 7 3 2　　(3) ♡ A 9 7 3 2

　　 ♠ Q 10 9　　　　 ◇ Q 10 6 4　　　 ♡ Q 10 8 5

With (1) most textbooks recommend running the 10, to be followed by a second finesse. It is a better practical proposition to start with a low card from dummy. Many East players will plunge in with the king. Should East follow with a low card, you finesse ♠ 10 and later run ♠ Q for a second finesse.

With (2) you should cash ◇ A and then lead low to the 10. This is better than leading to the queen on the second round since it gains when East has ◇ K J x x.

If you need all five tricks on (3) there are, rather surprisingly, two possible chances. Leading ♡ A will win if West has a singleton king; leading ♡ Q will win if East has a singleton jack. When four tricks are the target the best practical chance is again to lead low from the ace. Only a top-class player will play low at an even pace from K x. If East does play low, you finesse the 10. Should this lose to the jack, run ♡ Q on the next round.

Many problems arise from combinations involving the ace, jack and 10. Check your play on these holdings before reading on:

(1) ♡ A J 6 2　　(2) ♣ A J 3　　(3) ◇ A J 6 5

　　 ♡ 10 5 3　　　　 ♣ 10 7 6 4　　　 ◇ 10 7 3 2

If you need three tricks on (1) you must lead low to the jack, hoping that West holds K Q x or K Q alone. If two tricks will suffice you should cash the ace, then lead towards the 10 (this fails only when West started with ♡ Q x or ♡ K x).

The second holding is similar. Seeking three tricks you lead low to the jack. When your target is just two tricks you cash ♣ A and lead towards ♣ J on the second round.

With (3) you can make three tricks if West holds K Q x, K Q, Q x or K x. Your first play is low towards the jack. If you need only two tricks you must guard against a singleton honour by cashing ◇ A first and then leading towards either honour.

Finessing to gain an entry

Sometimes you will finesse as part of some larger strategy – to gain an entry, for example.

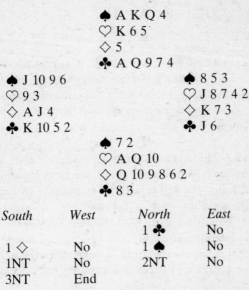

South	West	North	East
		1 ♣	No
1 ◇	No	1 ♠	No
1NT	No	2NT	No
3NT	End		

West leads ♠ J and you win in dummy. A diamond to the 10 loses to West's jack and ♠ 10 is continued. You win in dummy once more. What now?

The best shot is to finesse ♡ 10, seeking an extra entry to establish the diamonds. When this shrewd move proves successful, you drive out the defenders' second diamond stopper. Two heart entries remain, enabling you to clear the diamond suit and then enjoy the long cards.

The ruffing finesse

In trump contracts a special type of finesse becomes possible –
the ruffing finesse. These are typical positions:

(1) ♣ A Q J 10   (2) ♠ K J 9 3   (3) ♡ None

♣ 4   ♠ 1)   ♡ Q J 10 9

With (1) you cash ♣ A and lead ♣ Q. If East plays low, you
discard a loser from hand. If East covers with the king, you ruff
in hand, establishing two discards without losing a trick.

With (2) you start by running ♠ 10. If this loses to the queen,
you will run ♠ K on the next round, hoping that East has the
ace.

The final position is a *combination ruffing finesse*. Your first
move is to run ♡ Q, discarding a loser from dummy if West
plays low. Later you will repeat the manoeuvre by running the
jack. You score two tricks for the loss of one when the
defenders' honours are divided. Should West hold both the
high heart honours, you will score two tricks without loss.

Bearing this last combination in mind, take the helm in this
six-spade contract and see if you can spot the best line. West
leads ♣ J.

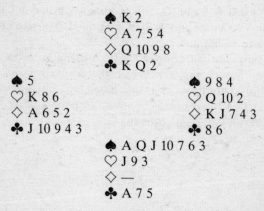

```
                    ♠ K 2
                    ♡ A 7 5 4
                    ◇ Q 10 9 8
                    ♣ K Q 2
♠ 5                                    ♠ 9 8 4
♡ K 8 6                                ♡ Q 10 2
◇ A 6 5 2                              ◇ K J 7 4 3
♣ J 10 9 4 3                          ♣ 8 6
                    ♠ A Q J 10 7 6 3
                    ♡ J 9 3
                    ◇ —
                    ♣ A 7 5
```

You have two losers in hearts. Your aim must be to park these losers on dummy's diamond suit, losing the lead only once in the process. For this play to succeed, you will need to find East with at least two of the three missing diamond honours (a 50% chance).

Win the club lead in dummy and play ♢ Q. If East covers with the king, you ruff in hand. Then play the ace and king of trumps and lead ♢ 10. East plays low, so you discard one of your losers from hand. West will win and doubtless return another club. You win in dummy and lead ♢ 9, leaving East with two unattractive options. If he covers, you will ruff and draw the last trump, then cross to ♡ A to discard your remaining heart loser. If East fails to cover, you will throw your remaining heart loser immediately.

The intra-finesse

Perhaps the most exotic form of finesse occurs on combinations such as these:

$$♡ Q 9 8 3$$
$$♡ 10\ 5 \qquad\qquad ♡ K J 4$$
$$♡ A 7 6 2$$

Lead a low heart towards dummy. If you place East with ♡ K, take a deep finesse of dummy's ♡ 9. East wins with the jack but on the next round you can lead ♡ Q from dummy, picking up East's king and pinning West's ten. Note that it would be less attractive to play ♡ A on the second round, hoping to drop the king. East is roughly twice as likely to hold ♡ K J x as ♡ K J alone. The term 'intra-finesse' was devised by the dextrous Brazilian player, Gabriel Chagas.

QUIZ ON FINESSING

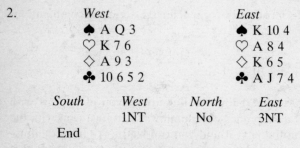

1.   West   East
           ♠ K 10 9 6 2   ♠ A Q 3
           ♡ A K J   ♡ 9 6 2
           ◇ A 5 3   ◇ Q J 7 2
           ♣ 10 8   ♣ A K 7

South	West	North	East
			1NT
No	3 ♠	No	4 ♣
No	4 ◇	No	4 ♠
No	5 ♡	No	6 ♠
End			

You reach six spades and North leads a low club. Plan the play.

2.   West   East
           ♠ A Q 3   ♠ K 10 4
           ♡ K 7 6   ♡ A 8 4
           ◇ A 9 3   ◇ K 6 5
           ♣ 10 6 5 2   ♣ A J 7 4

South	West	North	East
	1NT	No	3NT
End			

(a) North leads ♠ 2. Plan the play.

(b) North leads ♡ Q. Plan the play.

ANSWERS TO QUIZ

1. Win the lead and draw trumps, starting with ♠ A Q from dummy so that you can pick up a possible ♠ J x x x with South. You must now aim for three tricks in diamonds so that you won't need the heart finesse. It is pointless to lead ◇ Q from dummy. You would then need a 3–3 diamond break, wherever

the king was. Instead, lead a low diamond towards the Q J. If South wins with the king and switches to a heart, you will put up the ace and test the diamond suit before falling back on the heart finesse. If, instead, ♢ Q wins the trick, return to ♢ A and lead a third round of diamonds towards the jack.

2.(a) You need only two club tricks and you can afford to lose the lead twice more. Win the opening lead and play ♣ A to guard against a singleton honour with South. If the ace draws only small cards, continue by leading a club towards either the jack or the 10. This line of play will succeed however the club suit lies.

(b) On a heart lead you have less time and must play differently. Best is to win with ♡ K and lead low to ♣ J.

ESTABLISHING SUITS IN DUMMY

When you are planning to throw losers on a long suit in dummy your general plan will be: (1) draw trumps; (2) establish dummy's suit, if necessary; and (3) cross to dummy to take the discards.

Sometimes entries to dummy may be scarce and you may need to establish the side suit first. This is the type of hand we have in mind:

```
                    ♠ Q 5 4
                    ♡ 7 2
                    ◇ A K 9 7 6 2
                    ♣ A Q
  ♠ 10 8 2                         ♠ 7 6
  ♡ K 9 4                          ♡ Q 8 6 5 3
  ◇ J 5 4                          ◇ Q 10
  ♣ 9 8 7 4                        ♣ K J 6 3
                    ♠ A K J 9 3
                    ♡ A J 10
                    ◇ 8 3
                    ♣ 10 5 2
```

South	West	North	East
1 ♠	No	2 ◇	No
2 ♠	No	4 ♣	No
4 ♡	No	6 ♠	End

You reach a sound six-spade contract and ♣ 9 is led. The finesse loses and East returns another club. You cash the ace and king of diamonds and ruff a diamond, establishing the suit. You now play three rounds of trumps, ending in dummy. Finally you discard two hearts and a club on dummy's three good diamonds.

On the next hand you have a loser in the suit you want to establish. How would you plan the play?

```
                    ♠ 9 7 2
                    ♡ 8 3
                    ◇ K 8
                    ♣ A 9 7 6 5 2
    ♠ Q J 10 3                      ♠ 8 6 4
    ♡ 10 7 4 2                      ♡ 5
    ◇ Q 7 2                         ◇ J 10 9 5 4 3
    ♣ Q 10                          ♣ K J 4
                    ♠ A K 5
                    ♡ A K Q J 9 6
                    ◇ A 6
                    ♣ 8 3
```

South	West	North	East
2 ♣	No	3 ♣	No
3 ♡	No	3NT	No
4NT	No	5 ◇	No
5NT	No	6 ◇	No
6 ♡	End		

West leads ♠ Q against six hearts. Looking at the losers in the long trump hand, you see an unavoidable loser in clubs and a further loser in spades that will have to be discarded on dummy's club suit.

You win the spade lead and draw trumps in four rounds. Now what? If you play ace and another club you can enter dummy later with ◇ K to ruff the clubs good, but there will be no further entry to enjoy them. Since one club trick must be lost anyway, it makes good sense to give up the first round of clubs. You can then win the return in hand, cross to the ace of clubs and ruff the suit good. Finally you will cross to ◇ K to take your discard. This type of play, ducking an early round, is often used when establishing suits in notrumps, as we will see later.

Sometimes it may take two ruffs to establish a suit, as on this type of hand:

```
                    ♠ A 8
                    ♡ 9 6 4
                    ◇ K 10
                    ♣ A Q 8 6 5 2
   ♠ J 9 7 5 3                      ♠ 10 6 4 2
   ♡ J 8 5                          ♡ Q 10 7 3
   ◇ 8 5 4 2                        ◇ 6
   ♣ 9                              ♣ K J 10 3
                    ♠ K Q
                    ♡ A K 2
                    ◇ A Q J 9 7 3
                    ♣ 7 4
```

South	West	North	East
		1 ♣	No
2 ◇	No	3 ♣	No
3 ◇	No	4 ◇	No
4NT	No	5 ♡	No
5NT	No	6 ◇	End

West leads ♣ 9 against six diamonds. Anxious not to suffer a ruff, you win with dummy's ace. You must now aim to discard your heart loser on dummy's club suit.

Realizing that you will need dummy's trump honours as entries, you play a second round of clubs immediately. East wins and switches to a spade, which you take in hand, preserving the ace as a later entry to dummy. You now cross to ◇ 10 and ruff a club with the ace. Next you cross to ◇ K and ruff a club with the queen, establishing the club suit. It only remains to draw trumps and cross to ♠ A to discard your heart loser on a good club.

When declarer is attempting to set up a long suit in dummy, the defenders must try to thwart him by attacking the entries to dummy. Take the East cards on this hand:

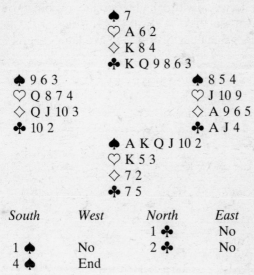

	South	West	North	East
			1 ♣	No
	1 ♠	No	2 ♣	No
	4 ♠	End		

West, your partner, leads ♢ Q against four spades and you press on with two more rounds of the suit. Declarer ruffs the third round and draws trumps. He now leads a club to the king, hoping in time to establish a discard for his heart loser.

If you win the trick and attempt to knock out dummy's entry by leading ♡ J, you will be disappointed. Declarer will win the heart in hand, cross to ♣ Q and ruff the clubs good. He will then enter dummy with ♡ A to discard his heart loser.

Instead you should allow ♣ K to win. This deprives declarer of a subsequent club entry and dooms the contract to failure.

But what if declarer has just a singleton club and maybe ♡ K x x x? Wouldn't ducking the ace of clubs give him the contract then? Indeed it would. But partner will help you on these occasions by giving you a count on his own holding in the key suit. With an EVEN number of clubs he will play a HIGH card on the first round. With an ODD number of clubs he will play a LOW card. So, on the present hand your partner should play the 10 on the first round of clubs. That will mark him (and therefore declarer) with a doubleton club, enabling you to duck the club without risk. We will look further at the important technique of signalling distribution in a later chapter.

QUIZ ON ESTABLISHING SUITS

1.

	West		East
	♠ K 8 2		♠ A 7 3
	♡ A K Q J 10		♡ 7 6 2
	◇ 8 3		◇ A K 9 7 2
	♣ A K 5		♣ J 3

South	West	North	East
			1 ◇
No	2 ♡	No	3 ◇
No	3 ♡	No	4 ♡
No	4NT	No	5 ♡
No	5NT	No	6 ◇
No	7 ♡	End	

Partner surprises you by opening the bidding and you drive to the grand slam in hearts. North leads ♠ Q. You win with the king and cash two rounds of trumps. How do you continue
  (a) if hearts are 3–2?
  (b) if hearts are 4–1?

2.

	West		East
	♠ K Q J 10 3		♠ A 2
	♡ A K 5		♡ 9 7 3
	♢ A 2		♢ 10 8 5
	♣ 8 5 3		♣ A 9 7 6 2

South	West	North	East
	1 ♠	No	1NT
No	3 ♠	No	4 ♠
End			

Perhaps the 100 honours tempted you to rebid three spades. Anyhow, you miss the best contract of 3NT and arrive in four spades. North leads ♡ Q. Plan the play.

3.

	North
	♠ A 5
	♡ A 7 4
	♢ 8 6 2
	♣ K Q 9 8 5

	East
	♠ 9 4 3
♢ Q led	♡ J 8 6 2
	♢ 9 4 3
	♣ A J 7

South	West	North	East
1 ♠	No	2 ♣	No
3 ♠	No	4 ♡	No
4NT	No	5 ♡	No
6 ♠	End		

South plays in six spades and West (your partner) leads ♢ Q. Declarer wins with the king and immediately leads ♣ 4. Your partner plays ♣ 6 and dummy the king. Plan the defence.

1.(a) If hearts are 3–2, play two rounds of diamonds and ruff a diamond. If these don't break, ruff a club and ruff another diamond, establishing a discard for your spade loser.

(b) If hearts are 4–1, you should draw the remaining trumps immediately. You will then need the diamond suit to break 3–3.

2. You should plan to establish the club suit to discard one of your red-suit losers. Win the heart lead, draw trumps and duck a round of clubs. Win the red-suit return and duck a second round of clubs. The defenders can now cash whichever winner they have established, but you will be able to discard your other loser on dummy's clubs (provided they broke 3–2). By ducking clubs twice you preserve ♣ A as an entry.

3. Partner's ♣ 6 suggests that he holds four cards in the suit. Declarer therefore holds a singleton and it would be unwise for you to hold off ♣ A. After winning the first round of clubs, no heroics are called for. You can see that declarer has insufficient entries to establish and enjoy the clubs. You should therefore exit safely in diamonds. To switch to hearts, in a misguided attempt to knock out dummy's ♡ A, might cost the contract if declarer held ♡ K 10 9.

4

RUFFING IN THE DUMMY

When you are planning to ruff losers in the dummy, it is usually impractical to draw trumps first. You may therefore need to take steps to avoid being overruffed. Should you ruff low and risk an overruff? Or should you ruff high, weakening your trump holding? You may also have to decide how many rounds of trumps to draw before taking the ruff. This is the type of hand we have in mind:

West	*East*
♠ A Q 6 2	♠ K 3
♡ A K J 7 3	♡ Q 9 2
◇ 8 5	◇ A K 7 6
♣ 6 5	♣ A K 9 4

Sitting West, you play in seven hearts on a minor-suit lead. The obvious line of play is to ruff the third round of spades. If you ruff with the queen, you will lose a trump trick when one of the defenders holds ♡ 10 x x x. If, instead, you play ace and queen of trumps before taking the ruff, you will fail when either defender can ruff the third round of spades with ♡ 10.

Best play is to ruff the spade with dummy's ♡ 9, without drawing any trumps first. This will succeed when North holds a doubleton spade, also when South holds a doubleton spade but not ♡ 10.

Your play on the next hand will depend on whether you are in six spades or seven.

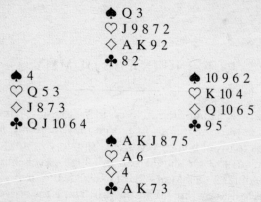

West leads ♣ Q against your spade slam. In a grand slam you would ruff the third round of clubs low and the fourth round with the queen. You would then need a 3–2 trump break.

This would not be the right play in a small slam. On the above layout East would overruff the third round of clubs and return a trump, leaving you one trick short. To prevent such a disaster, you should take your first ruff with the queen. You can then cash ♦ A K, throwing a heart, and return to ♡ A. Now you ruff your last club with ♠ 3. East is welcome to overruff, but the contract is secure.

Do you normally draw trumps straight away unless you need an early ruff in the dummy? Careful! You may find you need a not-so-early ruff. What do you make of this hand, played in four spades?

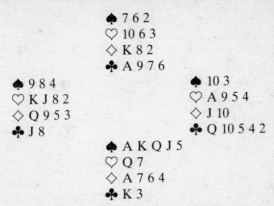

♠ 7 6 2
♡ 10 6 3
◇ K 8 2
♣ A 9 7 6

♠ 9 8 4   ♠ 10 3
♡ K J 8 2   ♡ A 9 5 4
◇ Q 9 5 3   ◇ J 10
♣ J 8   ♣ Q 10 5 4 2

♠ A K Q J 5
♡ Q 7
◇ A 7 6 4
♣ K 3

West leads ♡ 2 against four spades. The defenders persevere
with the suit and you ruff the third round. The contract will
easily succeed if diamonds break 3–3. If they are 4–2, which is
more likely, you may be able to ruff the fourth round if the
defender with the doubleton diamond has only two trumps.

Suppose you draw two rounds of trumps, then play ace, king
and a third diamond. This will not be good enough. The
defender on play will either lead a third round of trumps (as in
the present layout), or his partner will be able to overruff the
fourth round of diamonds.

Try something else. Duck the first round of diamonds! You
can then win the return, draw two rounds of trumps and play
◇ A K. If diamonds were 3–3 all the time, you will simply draw
the last trump. On the present hand diamonds are 4–2 but you
can ruff the fourth round successfully. The principle is an
important one. When you will have to give up a trick in a suit,
do it when the defenders can cause the least damage.

You can often establish a ruffing situation by discarding
side-suit losers from dummy.

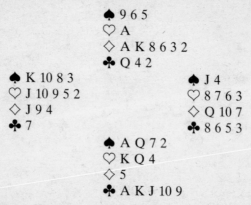

♠ 9 6 5
♡ A
◇ A K 8 6 3 2
♣ Q 4 2

♠ K 10 8 3
♡ J 10 9 5 2
◇ J 9 4
♣ 7

♠ J 4
♡ 8 7 6 3
◇ Q 10 7
♣ 8 6 5 3

♠ A Q 7 2
♡ K Q 4
◇ 5
♣ A K J 10 9

West leads ♡ J against your grand slam in clubs. You cross to
♠ A and discard two of dummy's spades on ♡ K Q. Then you
ruff a spade, return to ♣ A and ruff another spade with the club
queen. Next you cash ◇ A K, discarding your last spade. Your
last four cards are ♣ K J 10 9. Time to draw trumps!

On the next hand the fall of the cards suggests that an
overruff is imminent. By swapping one ruff for another you can
keep the defenders at bay.

♠ 7 6 3
♡ 7 4
◇ K 10 9 6 5
♣ 8 5 4

♠ 9 2
♡ K Q 10 9 6 5
◇ Q 8 2
♣ J 10

♠ 10 5 4
♡ A 3
◇ J 7 4
♣ Q 9 7 3 2

♠ A K Q J 8
♡ J 8 2
◇ A 3
♣ A K 6

You play in four spades and West leads ♡ K. East overtakes
with the ace and returns a heart to West's nine. West continues
with ♡ Q.

The defenders' antics suggest the hearts may be 6–2. If you believe this, you will discard a club on the third round of hearts. You can then win the return, draw two rounds of trumps and ruff a club in dummy. By throwing one loser on another you swap a dangerous heart ruff for what you hope will prove a safer club ruff. This technique of exchanging one ruff for another is known as 'trading ruffs'.

QUIZ ON RUFFING IN THE DUMMY

1.
	West	*East*
♠	A K Q 7 2	8 5 3
♡	10 8	K 6
♢	A Q 8 3	7 6 4
♣	K 4	A 9 8 5 2

You reach four spades and North leads ♡ Q. The defenders take two tricks in the suit and switch to a trump. Plan the play.

2.
	West	*East*
♠	A K 8 5	7 3
♡	K 9 2	A 8 4
♢	6	Q 8 7 5 2
♣	A K Q J 9	7 5 2

3NT would have been easy but you find yourself in five clubs. North leads ♢ 3 to South's jack and a low diamond is returned. Plan the play.

ANSWERS TO QUIZ

1. You must aim to take the diamond finesse at some stage and to ruff the fourth round of diamonds if the suit does not divide 3–3. Since you must lose a trick in diamonds anyhow, it makes good sense to surrender it immediately. So, win the trump switch and lead a low diamond from hand. You plan to enter dummy, finesse ◇ Q, draw a second round of trumps and play ◇ A. If diamonds are 4–2, you will be able to ruff the fourth round successfully, provided the last trump lies with the four diamonds.

2. You have five trump tricks and four more winners in the side suits. You therefore need two ruffs in dummy to make the contract. Ruff the diamond return, cash ♠ A K and ruff a spade. Now play ♡ A K and lead the fourth spade. If North ruffs in front of the dummy, you can discard dummy's heart loser and later ruff a heart (with dummy's ♣ 7 to reduce the risk of an overruff). If, instead, North follows on the fourth round of spades, then your best chance is to throw the heart loser. If South started with four hearts, or three hearts and no club higher than the 7, you will be able to score a heart ruff.

5

PLANNING A NOTRUMP CONTRACT

Notrump contracts often develop into a straightforward race between the two sides. The defenders are first off the blocks and declarer may have to outwit them if he is to reach the tape first.

Here is a fairly straightforward 3NT contract. How would you plan the play?

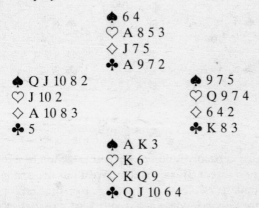

West leads ♠ Q against 3NT and it is advisable to win immediately (otherwise you give them a chance to switch to hearts with a trick in the bag). Clubs are the most promising source of tricks and it may seem natural to attack this suit first. But see what happens if you do. East will win and clear the spade suit. When you try for a ninth trick in diamonds, West will fly in with the ace and cash his spade winners to put you one down.

When, as on the present hand, you have two enemy stoppers to knock out, it is often important to attack them in the right

order. You should aim first at the stopper that lies with the long
cards in the defenders' suit. In this case, West's only potential
card of entry is ♢ A, so you should play on diamonds first. Lead
♢ K. If West wins with ♢ A and continues spades, you must
duck. He will doubtless press on with spades but East will have
none left when you eventually take a losing club finesse.

The next hand is slightly different. You reach 3NT and West
leads ♠ 6 to East's king. Would you hold up or not?

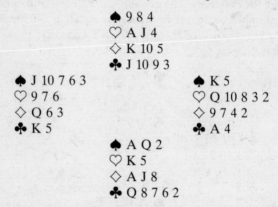

```
                    ♠ 9 8 4
                    ♡ A J 4
                    ♢ K 10 5
                    ♣ J 10 9 3
   ♠ J 10 7 6 3                   ♠ K 5
   ♡ 9 7 6                        ♡ Q 10 8 3 2
   ♢ Q 6 3                        ♢ 9 7 4 2
   ♣ K 5                          ♣ A 4
                    ♠ A Q 2
                    ♡ K 5
                    ♢ A J 8
                    ♣ Q 8 7 6 2
```

You must certainly hold up, because a switch to a different
suit poses no threat. If, as you fear, West has five spades, then
East will have a doubleton. By holding up on the first round and
winning the second, you will exhaust East's spades. You will
then be able to establish the club suit at leisure. West is
welcome to clear the spades; he will never get in to enjoy them.

If you had won the first round of spades, of course, things
would have been different. East would make sure to win the
first club trick and fire back his remaining spade. West would
then take his spade winners when in with ♣ K.

It is often clear, especially at notrumps, that one defender
must be kept out of the lead. This defender is described as the
danger hand. You must plan to establish your tricks without
letting him into the lead.

```
                    ♠ A 5
                    ♡ Q J 7
                    ◇ 9 7 6 5
                    ♣ A 10 4 3
♠ K Q 10 7 3                        ♠ 8 6 4
♡ K 8 6 4                           ♡ 10 9 5 2
◇ —                                 ◇ Q J 4
♣ Q 9 6 2                           ♣ J 8 7
                    ♠ J 9 2
                    ♡ A 3
                    ◇ A K 10 8 3 2
                    ♣ K 5
```

You open an off-beat 1NT and partner raises to game. West leads ♠ K, which you win in dummy. Since you need only five diamond tricks for game and don't mind West gaining the lead, you should immediately finesse ◇ 10. This play guarantees the contract against any distribution.

If, perish the thought, you play a diamond to the ace instead, there will be no second chance. East will gain the lead in diamonds and play a spade through your tenace.

Declarer made an early mistake on the next deal and found he could not recover.

```
                    ♠ A 9 6
                    ♡ 8 7 3
                    ◇ A J 6 5
                    ♣ K J 5
♠ J 8 2                            ♠ Q 7 4 3
♡ A J 9 5 2                        ♡ 10 6
◇ 9 4                              ◇ Q 10 2
♣ 9 7 3                            ♣ 10 8 6 2
                    ♠ K 10 5
                    ♡ K Q 4
                    ◇ K 8 7 3
                    ♣ A Q 4
```

Defending against 3NT, West led ♡ 5 to the 10 and queen. Declarer needed to develop the diamonds without letting East (the danger hand) into the lead. He therefore played ace, king and another diamond, guarding against a doubleton queen with East. This belated effort was not rewarded. East won the third round of diamonds and returned a heart to put the game one down.

Do you see how declarer could have made the contract? By letting East's ♡ 10 win the first trick he could have broken the link between the defenders' hands. They would doubtless clear the heart suit but it would be a simple matter to establish an extra diamond trick without letting West, now the danger hand, into the lead.

A hold-up is often declarer's first manoeuvre in a notrump contract. There is no reason why it should be his last, though. Many players would go down in the next 3NT contract.

```
              ♠ Q J 8 2
              ♡ 7 4
              ♢ K Q 2
              ♣ A 10 8 4
  ♠ A 7 3                      ♠ 10 9 6 4
  ♡ K Q J 10 3                 ♡ 8 6 5
  ♢ 8 4                        ♢ 9 7 3
  ♣ Q J 7                      ♣ 9 6 3
              ♠ K 5
              ♡ A 9 2
              ♢ A J 10 6 5
              ♣ K 5 2
```

South	West	North	East
1NT	No	2 ♣	No
2 ♢	No	3NT	End

West leads ♡ K against 3NT. After holding up hearts for two rounds, you could play a spade. This would win if East held ♣ A or if hearts were 4–4. But why not run the diamonds first?

There is nothing to lose as far as you are concerned and the
defender with the long hearts may come under pressure. West
will need to find three discards. Two will be painless; the third
will not. If he throws a heart, it will be quite safe for you to
knock out the spade ace.

Holding up your stopper in the enemy suit is not always the
best tactic. Sometimes the early release of a high card will block
the defenders' suit. Look at this example:

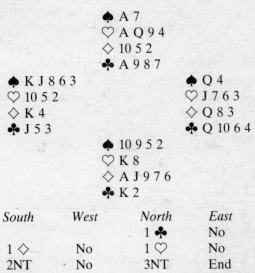

	♠ A 7	
	♡ A Q 9 4	
	◇ 10 5 2	
	♣ A 9 8 7	

♠ K J 8 6 3		♠ Q 4
♡ 10 5 2		♡ J 7 6 3
◇ K 4		◇ Q 8 3
♣ J 5 3		♣ Q 10 6 4

	♠ 10 9 5 2	
	♡ K 8	
	◇ A J 9 7 6	
	♣ K 2	

South	West	North	East
		1 ♣	No
1 ◇	No	1 ♡	No
2NT	No	3NT	End

West loses no time in leading ♠ 6. If you play low from
dummy, East will win with the queen and clear the suit. The
situation will be hopeless. Instead, you must play dummy's ♠ A
at trick one, blocking the defenders' spades. A diamond to the
jack loses to West's king. West crosses to his partner's ♠ Q, but
the spade suit is dead. When you regain the lead you will play
ace and another diamond, not risking the finesse.

This type of blocking play is possible with several other combinations:

♡ A 8 2

♡ K 10 7 6 3   ♡ Q 5

♡ J 9 4

West leads ♡ 6 against 3NT. If the key finesse is into the West hand, your best play is to rise with dummy's ♡ A at trick one. East may decide to unblock the queen, but West will be unable to continue the suit when he gains the lead.

QUIZ ON PLANNING NOTRUMP CONTRACTS

1.

West	East
♠ A J 6	♠ 8 4
♡ A 8 3	♡ K 9 7 6
◇ Q J 4	◇ K 10 9 6 3
♣ A 10 8 2	♣ K 4

Love all

South	West	North	East
	1 ♣	No	1 ◇
No	1NT	No	3NT
End			

North leads ♠ 5 against your 3NT contract and South plays the queen. Plan the play.

2.

West	East
♠ A 9 2	♠ J 4
♡ 8 6 3	♡ A K 9
◇ A K 4	◇ Q 8 3
♣ A J 7 6	♣ Q 10 9 5 2

South	West	North	East
	1NT	No	3NT
End			

North leads ♠ 6 against 3NT. Plan the play.

3.

	West		East
	♠ A Q 3		♠ 10 7 2
	♡ 9 7 6 2		♡ A 4
	◇ J 8 4		◇ K Q 10 9 6 2
	♣ A K 9		♣ Q 5

South	West	North	East
	1NT	No	3NT
End			

North leads ♡ 5 against 3NT. Plan the play.

ANSWERS TO QUIZ

1. If North holds ◇ A you must win the spade ace immediately. Your ♠ J x will then stop the suit a second time. If South holds ◇ A, the situation is different. You must hold up ♠ A for two rounds to exhaust South of the suit.

So, who has ◇ A? Think back to the bidding. If North had held five or six spades to the king, an honour or two in hearts and clubs *and* the ace of diamonds, he might have overcalled in spades. This is enough to tilt the odds in favour of playing South for the diamond ace. You should therefore hold up the spade ace for two rounds.

2. You should play ♠ J from dummy at trick one, in case North has underled the K Q. Playing low can never gain.

If South covers ♠ J, you should duck the trick. Duck the spade continuation also and win the third round with the ace. North is now the danger hand. Since you need only four club tricks, you should not risk losing a club finesse to the singleton king. Play ♣ A at trick four, then another club. You don't mind losing a trick to ♣ K with South, since if he has a spade left the suit will be 4–4.

3. If North has led from a five-card heart suit and South has the diamond ace, a simple hold-up in hearts will succeed. The alternative play is to win the first trick with dummy's heart ace, hoping that South has a doubleton such as ♡ Q 10, which will

block the defenders' hearts. Since North would doubtless have led an honour if his hearts were headed by K Q J, K Q 10, K J 10 or Q J 10, the chances of a block are excellent. You should therefore go up with the ace of hearts at trick one and attack the diamond suit.

6

OPENING LEAD IN NOTRUMP CONTRACTS

When leading against notrump contracts, you will often look no further than 'fourth best from your longest and strongest'. Remember, though, that the object is to find the most constructive lead for the *partnership*, not just for your hand. Assuming that the bidding has been an uninformative 1NT–3NT, what would you lead from these hands?

(1) ♠A94	(2) ♠Q842	(3) ♠A1082	(4) ♠Q9742
♡J108	♡953	♡54	♡J4
◇KJ852	◇A104	◇Q1086	◇1093
♣84	♣862	♣763	♣742

On (1) there is insufficient reason to shun a long-suit lead. Fire away with ◇ 5. It may give away a trick, but the prospects of establishing some long cards compensate for this. Against a final contract of 2NT there would be a better case for the give-nothing-away lead of ♡ J.

On the second hand the risk of leading the empty spade suit outweighs the possible gain. A four-card suit is considerably less promising than a five-carder. A better prospect here is to lead ♡ 9 or ♣ 8. Since responder might hold four clubs but would doubtless have bid Stayman with four hearts, ♡ 9 may prove the best shot.

Hand (3) contains two reasonable four-card suits worth leading. As we mentioned on the previous hand, it is often preferable to lead a major suit rather than a minor. Here, though, ◇ 6 is the more promising lead since ♠ A may subsequently provide an entry if the diamonds can be established.

Hand (4) has no side entry, so even if the spade suit could be set up it is unlikely that you would ever gain the lead to enjoy the suit. Try leading ◇ 10 instead. You won't give much away and you may hit partner's long suit. Also, you retain a better possibility of making a trick with ♠ Q.

Which card should you lead?

When you have decided the suit to lead, the problem of which card to lead is usually not difficult. This is the general scheme when leading against notrumps:

1. From a sequence of honours, such as A K Q or K Q J, lead the top card.
2. From a 'broken sequence', such as A K J or K Q 10, again lead the top card.
3. From an 'interior sequence', such as A Q J or K J 10, lead the middle honour.
4. Otherwise lead fourth best from any suit containing an honour. Lead the 4 from K 10 6 4 or K 9 8 4 2. From three to an honour lead the bottom card – the 3 from Q 7 3.
5. From four small cards lead the second highest and follow with the bottom card on the next round. From 8 6 5 2 lead the 6, then play the 2.
6. From two or three small cards, lead the top one and follow with the next highest on the second round. Lead the 6 from 6 5 2 and follow with the 5.

When should you experiment?

Sometimes there is a good case for an unorthodox lead. What would you lead here?

West holds:

$$\spadesuit \text{ K Q J 7 2}$$
$$\heartsuit \text{ A 6 4}$$
$$\diamondsuit \text{ 10 8}$$
$$\clubsuit \text{ 9 5 3}$$

South	North
	1 ♡
1 ♠	2 ◇
3NT	

A spade lead is the best prospect despite South's bid in the suit. Don't lead the king, though. This will block the suit when your partner holds ♠ 10 x (or even ♠ A x). Lead a low card! Even if declarer holds ♠ A 10, you may hit the jackpot. This might be the full deal:

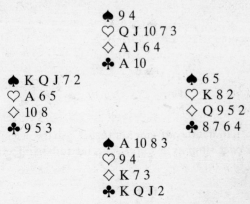

If you lead ♠ K, declarer will duck and succeed against any continuation. The link between you and your partner will be broken.

If you lead a low spade instead, declarer will win the trick cheaply. But whether he plays on hearts or diamonds, East will win and clear the spade suit.

The best lead from suits such as K 10 9 x x or Q 10 9 x x is not clear-cut. Although textbooks advise the 10, the low card is often better when you suspect one opponent may hold four cards in the suit.

Leading in special situations

When an opening bid of 3NT (signifying a long minor suit) is passed out, time is all-important. Which card would you lead here?

West holds:

♠ A 5 3
♡ Q J 10 5 3
♢ J 7 5 2
♣ 8

South	West	North	East
3NT	No	No	No

The queen of hearts can wait her turn. Cash the ace of spades first to inspect dummy's stoppers. The full hand might be something like this:

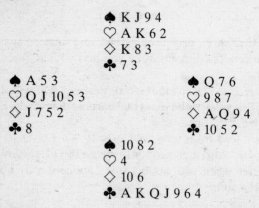

♠ K J 9 4
♡ A K 6 2
♢ K 8 3
♣ 7 3

♠ A 5 3
♡ Q J 10 5 3
♢ J 7 5 2
♣ 8

♠ Q 7 6
♡ 9 8 7
♢ A Q 9 4
♣ 10 5 2

♠ 10 8 2
♡ 4
♢ 10 6
♣ A K Q J 9 6 4

When dummy appears, it will be obvious that a diamond switch is required. Since you need to hold the lead if declarer ducks in dummy, your switch must be to the jack of diamonds, not a low one.

Another special situation occurs when partner doubles a freely bid 3NT contract. What do you make of partner's double here?

West holds:

♠ 7 3
♡ Q 8 6 5 2
♢ 10 9 7 3
♣ 10 4

South	West	North	East
1 ♣	No	1 ♠	No
2 ♣	No	3 ♣	No
3NT	No	No	dble
End			

Without the double you would attack in one of the red suits, probably leading ♡ 5. Partner's double suggests something different. It calls for the lead of dummy's first bid suit, spades in this instance. Perhaps he has ♠ K Q J 9 x and the ace of clubs.

Leading against notrump slams

When the opponents have reached a notrump slam, you should look for a safe lead. Give nothing away. Try this hand, for example:

West holds:

♠ Q 10 8 2
♡ 10 7
♢ 9 7 4 2
♣ 8 5 3

South	North
2NT	6NT

Leading a major suit is out of the question – much too dangerous. It is slightly safer to lead from four small cards than three, since declarer's own holdings in the suit are likely to be shorter. You should therefore try a low diamond. In general, the longer the suit, the less likely that a lead will assist declarer. For example, J x x x x is a safer lead than 10 x x.

The only time when you might make an attacking lead from a king or queen is in a pairs game, where declarer may have taken a gamble to play in the higher scoring contract.

QUIZ ON LEADING AGAINST NOTRUMP CONTRACTS

1. As West, you hold:

♠ A 8 2
♡ K 10 9 3
♢ 8 6 2
♣ K J 7

South	North
1NT	3NT

Which card would you choose if you decided to lead
(a) a spade?
(b) a heart?
(c) a diamond?
(d) a club?
2. What do you think is the best lead on the above hand?
3. As West, you hold:

♠ 5 3
♡ 8 4
♢ 9 7 5 2
♣ J 8 6 5 4

South	West	North	East
1 ♢	No	1 ♡	1 ♠
3 ♢	No	4 ♢	No
4NT	No	5 ♢	No
6NT	No	No	dble
End			

What do you understand by partner's double? Which card would you lead?

ANSWERS TO QUIZ

    1. (a) ♠ 2. Lowest card from three to an honour.

      (b) ♡ 10. The 10 9 form an interior sequence.

      (c) ♢ 8. Top of three small against notrumps.

      (d) ♣ J. To lead low would risk blocking the suit.

    2. Some players would lead ♢ 8, hoping to give nothing away, but subsequent discarding often becomes too difficult. Lead ♡ 10. You have a useful hand and every prospect of regaining the lead if the heart suit can be established.

    3. If partner wanted a spade lead he would pass 6NT and expect you to lead the suit he had bid. His double requests the lead of dummy's first bid suit. Perhaps he has ♡ A K, or ♡ A Q poised over the heart bidder, or ♡ K and a side trick. Lead ♡ 8. If instead you make the wooden lead of a spade declarer may run a rapid twelve tricks.

7

OPENING LEAD IN SUIT CONTRACTS

Although all opening leads are made somewhat in the dark, the bidding usually offers a clue or two. For example, if the opponents veer away from 3NT and play in five of a minor, it will usually pay you to attack the unbid suit. Even if you hold A x x x, be bold and lead out the ace. There's a good chance that partner holds the king.

Against trump contracts it is usually good tactics to make aggressive leads. This is particularly true when dummy has announced a side suit. What would you lead here?

West holds:

♠ 10 9 8
♡ K J 4
♢ K 10 7 5 3
♣ J 6

South	North
1 ♠	2 ♣
2 ♠	4 ♠

Don't lead a trump; declarer is more likely to set up the clubs than to play for ruffs. Fire away in one of the red suits. Hearts, the shorter suit, are the better prospect for establishing tricks, since the opponents are more likely to be short in diamonds.

Which card to lead?

Once you have decided which suit to lead, the card to choose is much the same as against notrump contracts (top of honour sequences and interior sequences, fourth best from broken suits. See Chapter 6). These are the main exceptions:

1. From a side suit headed by two touching honours, such as K Q x x or Q J x x or J 10 x x, lead the top honour rather than fourth best. Your aim now is to establish quick tricks. From A K x x the traditional lead is the king, but tournament players incline towards the ace. There are arguments both ways, and this is a matter you will need to settle with your partner.

2. Do not, in general, underlead a side-suit ace. If the bidding suggests a lead from a holding such as A x x or A x x x, lead the ace.

3. Three low cards, such as 8 6 4, present a problem. The 8 may seem to be from a doubleton. The 6, following a style known as MUD (middle-up-down), has one substantial disadvantage. Partner, holding perhaps A K x x, will not know until the second round (which may be too late) whether the lead is from two cards or three. The American practice of leading the bottom card is undoubtedly best, but this again is a matter on which there must be partnership agreement.

This is the type of hand where a MUD lead would pay dividends:

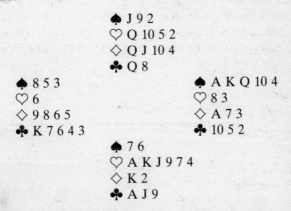

♠ J 9 2
♡ Q 10 5 2
♢ Q J 10 4
♣ Q 8

♠ 8 5 3   ♠ A K Q 10 4
♡ 6   ♡ 8 3
♢ 9 8 6 5   ♢ A 7 3
♣ K 7 6 4 3   ♣ 10 5 2

♠ 7 6
♡ A K J 9 7 4
♢ K 2
♣ A J 9

South plays in four hearts after East has mentioned his spade suit. West leads ♠ 5 and his partner wins the trick with the ten.

When East continues with ♠ A, West follows with ♠ 8.
Realizing that a spade continuation would be unproductive,
East switches to a club. The contract is now one down. Had
East not been sure of the spade situation and continued with
another spade, declarer would make the contract easily. He
would ruff, draw trumps and establish the diamond suit for two
discards.

When to experiment

West has a difficult lead on the following hand. Which card
would you choose?

West holds:

> ♠ A 8 2
> ♡ A 5
> ◇ J 8 7 2
> ♣ 10 6 5 4

	South	North
		2NT
	3 ♡	4 ♡

Leading from a jack is rarely profitable. Neither is a trump
lead very inviting from A x. You should therefore lead a black
suit. Since the high cards are amassed to your left, a low spade
lead may prove the best shot. The full hand may be something
like this:

                    ♠ K 9 4
                    ♡ Q J 3
                    ♢ A K 6 3
                    ♣ A K 9
    ♠ A 8 2   ♠ Q J 7 6
    ♡ A 5   ♡ 9 8 4
    ♢ J 8 7 2   ♢ 9 5
    ♣ 10 6 5 4   ♣ Q 8 7 2
                    ♠ 10 5 3
                    ♡ K 10 7 6 2
                    ♢ Q 10 4
                    ♣ J 3

If you lead ♠ 2, the unsuspecting declarer will doubtless play low from dummy and East's jack will win. East returns a trump to your ace and you continue blithely with ♠ 8. Declarer may go wrong now and try dummy's ♠ 9, giving the defenders three spades and a heart. Not only have you beaten an impregnable game, but this particular declarer will suspect all your honest leads in future.

The same ploy may be tried when dummy has opened a strong notrump. The lead is always a dangerous one, though, and the authors will not entertain letters of complaint should it occasionally misfire.

Here is another interesting tactical situation. Which card would you lead here?

West holds:

♠ 8 2
♡ K 9 7 6 2
♢ Q 7 2
♣ Q 6 5

South	West	North	East
			1 ♡
No	2 ♡	dble	No
2 ♠	No	3 ♠	No
4 ♠	End		

Your side is not likely to score more than one heart trick. The best lead is ♡ K, enabling you to hold the lead when partner has the ace. You can then inspect dummy, the strong hand, and decide on the best switch. This might be the full hand:

♠ A Q 5 4
♡ 5
♢ K 9 8
♣ A K J 8 3

♠ 8 2   ♠ 10
♡ K 9 7 6 2   ♡ A Q J 8 3
♢ Q 7 2   ♢ A J 10 4
♣ Q 6 5   ♣ 10 7 2

♠ K J 9 7 6 3
♡ 10 4
♢ 6 5 3
♣ 9 4

If you're clever enough to lead ♡ K, finding the ♢ Q switch should be no problem!

When to lead a trump

The old maxim 'when in doubt, lead a trump' is poorly conceived. Better advice would be 'when in doubt, attack an unbid side suit'. Mind you, there are situations in which a trump lead is indicated. Usually these are easy to recognize. What do you make of this auction?

West holds:

<pre>
         ♠ 9 6 2
         ♡ K 5
         ◇ Q 10 8 2
         ♣ 10 7 6 3
</pre>

South	North
1 ♣	2 ◇
2 ♡	2NT
3 ♡	3 ♠
4 ♣	No

When dummy has given reluctant preference to one of declarer's suits, a trump lead may prevent declarer ruffing his second suit good. Here you should lead ♣ 2. You plan to lead a second trump when in with ♡ K. If dummy is 2–2 in the majors, there are good chances of preventing declarer taking any ruffs. Note that it is more important to lead a trump when you hold K x in declarer's side suit than with a longer holding such as K J x x. The more cards you hold in the suit, the more chance that your partner can overruff the dummy.

Here are some other auctions to look for:

	South	North
(1)	1 ♠	1NT
	2 ♡	No

North may well be 1–3 in the majors. Always consider a trump lead when dummy has chosen to play in declarer's second suit.

	South	North
(2)	1NT	2 ♣
	2 ◇	No

Since North has passed the Stayman response of two diamonds, he must hold at least four cards in that suit. A trump lead is indicated.

	South	North
(3)	1 ♠	2 ♠
	3NT	4 ♠

South has offered an alternative spot, but North reckons that he will take a trick or two more in a trump contract. He is therefore counting on some ruffs in his hand. Perhaps a trump lead will prove the best defence.

Leading in special situations

One special situation arises when partner has doubled a freely bid slam. This will be a Lightner double, requesting an unusual lead, often the lead of dummy's first bid suit. What do you make of partner's double here?

West holds:

♠ Q J 10 4 2
♡ J 9 7 6
◇ 3
♣ 10 8 6

South	West	North	East
		1 ♡	No
2 ◇	No	3 ♣	No
3 ◇	No	4 ◇	No
4NT	No	5 ♡	No
6 ◇	No	No	dble

If your finger is on ♠ Q, remove it. Partner's double calls for the lead of one of dummy's suits. Is it hearts, the first bid suit, or perhaps clubs? There is a clue hidden in the auction. If partner had wanted a heart lead, he might well have doubled the five-heart Blackwood response. So, cross your fingers and lead ♣ 6. This might be the position:

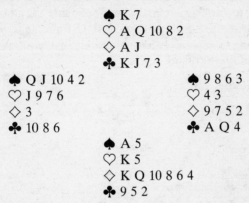

```
                        ♠ K 7
                        ♡ A Q 10 8 2
                        ♢ A J
                        ♣ K J 7 3
  ♠ Q J 10 4 2                        ♠ 9 8 6 3
  ♡ J 9 7 6                           ♡ 4 3
  ♢ 3                                 ♢ 9 7 5 2
  ♣ 10 8 6                            ♣ A Q 4
                        ♠ A 5
                        ♡ K 5
                        ♢ K Q 10 8 6 4
                        ♣ 9 5 2
```

What lead would be the most effective after this unusual auction?

West holds:

```
                        ♠ A Q 10 2
                        ♡ 9
                        ♢ K Q J 4
                        ♣ K 10 6 3
```

South	West	North	East
1 ♡	dble	No	No
No			

Why has your partner chosen to make hearts trumps? He must have a powerful holding such as K Q J x x or Q J 10 x x x. In that case it is essential to prevent declarer scoring ruffs with his low trumps. Lead ♡ 9 without delay. When partner gets in, he will continue to draw declarer's trumps. There will be plenty of time later to score your high cards in the side suits.

Leading against slams in a suit

When leading against a small slam in a suit, bare your teeth and be aggressive. Holdings such as K x x or Q x x are unattractive leads against a game, but they are close to the trigger when you are trying to gun down a small slam. Your side will gain the lead at most once more during the hand, so no time can be wasted in establishing a second defensive trick. Test your powers of aggression on this hand:

West holds:

♠ K 5 2
♡ Q 10 7 4
◇ 10 8 3
♣ K 8 2

South	West	North	East
1 ♠	No	3 ◇	No
3 ♠	No	4NT	No
5 ♡	No	6 ♠	End

You expect to gain the lead with ♠ K, so what is the best prospect of setting up a second trick? There are two reasons to try a club lead rather than a heart. In clubs you need only a queen from partner, whereas in hearts you must hope for greater riches – a king. Secondly, your hearts are longer. There is slightly more chance that the opponents can ruff the second round.

When your opponents bid a small slam and you hold an ace, do you cash it at trick 1 or not? Try this example:

West holds:

♠ Q 7 2
♡ J 9 8 3 2
♢ A 10 7
♣ K 3

South	West	North	East
		1 ♢	No
1 ♠	No	3 ♠	No
4NT	No	5 ♡	No
6 ♠	End		

As you are hopeful of scoring a trump trick, it makes good sense to cash ♢ A before the rats get at it. Or does it? Leading the ace of dummy's main suit may arouse declarer's suspicions. This might be the layout:

♠ A 10 9 4
♡ A 4
♢ K Q J 9 5
♣ Q 7

♠ Q 7 2   ♠ 6
♡ J 9 8 3 2   ♡ 10 7 6
♢ A 10 7   ♢ 8 6 3 2
♣ K 3   ♣ 10 9 6 5 4

♠ K J 8 5 3
♡ K Q 5
♢ 4
♣ A J 8 2

If you lead ♢ A, establishing discards for declarer's heart and club losers, it will be all too obvious that you are hoping for a trump trick. Declarer is likely to finesse against your queen of spades. The best lead is ♡ 3. Left to his own devices, declarer is destined to lose two tricks.

However, this was rather a special situation. In general, and when in doubt, don't be afraid to lead aces against small slams. It is unfortunate if this gives the contract, but positively humiliating to find that the ace, either at once or in time, would have produced two simple tricks.

QUIZ ON OPENING LEADS AGAINST SUIT CONTRACTS

1. You (West) hold:

♠ J 10 3
♡ 9 7 3
♢ Q J 5 2
♣ A 9 4

South	West	North	East
1 ♠	No	3 ♠	No
4 ♠	End		

Which card would you choose if you decided to lead:
(a) a spade?
(b) a heart?
(c) a diamond?
(d) a club?

2. What do you think is the best lead on the hand above?

3. You (West) hold:

♠ 9 7 6
♡ A 3
♢ J 9 7 6 2
♣ 9 6 5

South	West	North	East
		3 ♢	No
3 ♡	No	4 ♡	No
4NT	No	5 ♣	No
6 ♡	End		

Which lead is the best prospect here?

4. You (West) hold:

♠ 9 2
♡ K Q 7
♢ A Q J 9 4
♣ K Q 5

South	West	North	East
	1 ♢	No	1 ♡
1 ♠	3 ♡	No	4 ♡
No	No	4 ♠	dble
End			

The opponents have sacrificed at favourable vulnerability. What's the best lead?

ANSWERS TO QUIZ

1.(a) ♠ 3. Leading ♠ J may cost a trick if partner has a singleton queen or king.

(b) ♡ 7. On this occasion the 7 is probably best. You are not likely to find partner with A K, and if he wins the trick, say with the ace, you want him to switch to a minor suit.

(c) ♢ Q. Against a notrump contract you might lead ♢ 2. Against four spades you must lead an honour.

(d) ♣ A. If you underlead the ace, you may never make it. No heroics are called for here.

2. A club lead is far too dangerous. Even a low trump lead may cost a trick if partner has K x or A x. The diamond queen might work well, but a neutral heart lead is probably best. Give nothing away.

3. Has partner a void diamond? No, or he would have made a Lightner double. So you must choose a black suit lead. Since partner *might* have doubled the five-club response with a holding such as ♣ K Q, but had no chance to double a spade bid, the odds are slightly in favour of leading a spade.

4. You have the side suits well covered. Lead a trump to minimize the opponents' ruffs.

8

INFERENCES FROM THE OPENING LEAD

No doubt you have heard of the Rule of Eleven. Don't treat it as a curiosity – make use of it. When partner has led fourth best, subtract the pip value of his opening lead from 11. This will tell you how many higher cards in the suit the other three players hold.

An example will make this clear.

                   ♣ Q 10 3

♣ A K 8 6 4   ♣ 9 7

                   ♣ J 5 2

You are sitting East and partner leads ♣ 6 against 3NT. Six from eleven is five, so the other three players hold five clubs higher than the 6. Since you and the dummy hold four of them, declarer can hold only one. Declarer plays low from dummy and your ♣ 9 forces the jack. You now know that partner's clubs are headed by the A K and are ready to run.

Sometimes you may reach a quite different conclusion.

                   ♣ K 8 7

♣ 6 led   ♣ Q 5 3

Once again your partner leads ♣ 6, suggesting that declarer has only one higher card in the suit. You play the queen and declarer wins with the ace. It is time to reassess the position. Partner would not have led the 6 from ♣ J 10 9 6, so his lead cannot be fourth best. He must have led from ♣ 6 4 2, or possibly ♣ 9 6 4 2.

This kind of deduction helped East to beat 3NT on the following hand:

♠ Q J 9 3
♡ J 6 3
◇ Q 9
♣ A 10 7 4

♠ 8 6 5   ♠ A 7 2
♡ K 8 4   ♡ 9 7 5
◇ 7 4 3   ◇ A 10 8 6 2
♣ J 9 6 3   ♣ Q 5

♠ K 10 4
♡ A Q 10 2
◇ K J 5
♣ K 8 2

South	West	North	East
1 ♡	No	1 ♠	No
1NT	No	3 ♡	No
3 ♠	No	3NT	End

West made the happy lead of ◇ 7 against 3NT. Since East could see five cards higher than the seven, he realized that his partner's lead was 'top of nothing'. He therefore ducked when declarer put on dummy's queen, contenting himself with the 8, an encouraging signal.

Declarer knocked out the ace of spades and East returned a low diamond, keeping his ace as a subsequent re-entry. Declarer won, cashed the spade suit and continued with a heart finesse, which lost to West's king. West led back his last diamond and East cashed three tricks in the suit to put the contract one down.

In third position you must be wary of playing a high card which will surrender your entire defence in the suit led.

◇ A 10 2

◇ K 9 5 4   ◇ J 6 3

◇ Q 8 7

Less inspired than in the previous example, your partner leads ◇ 4 against a major-suit game. Declarer plays low from dummy. Since partner wouldn't underlead a king-queen against a suit contract, it is pointless to play your jack. Declarer will win and subsequently finesse dummy's ten, scoring three tricks in the suit.

Instead, play low at trick one. Declarer will win cheaply, but two tricks will be his limit in the suit unless he can engineer an end-play.

This is another position where third hand must avoid a trap:

$$♡ \text{ Q } 8$$

$$♡ \text{ 5 led} \qquad\qquad ♡ \text{ K } 10\ 7\ 2$$

After bidding of 1NT–3NT, your partner leads ♡ 5. Declarer plays low from dummy and you must decide whether to play the 10 or the king. The Rule of Eleven marks declarer with one card higher than the 5. If it is the jack, you must put on your king or you might suffer the indignity of allowing declarer to win a trick with J x. If it is the ace, you must play your 10 at trick one.

Many players reach automatically for the 10 in this position, reasoning that South opened the bidding and is therefore more likely to hold the missing ace. This is quite wrong. If declarer did hold the ace, he would have played the queen from dummy at trick one. Since he has not done so, you should place him with the jack and therefore play your king.

When it is clear that partner has led from a weak suit, third hand must consider whether or not it is wise to contribute a high card.

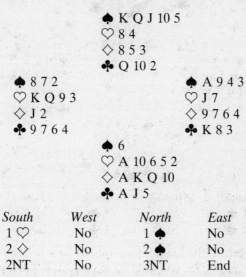

	♠ K Q J 10 5	
	♡ 8 4	
	◇ 8 5 3	
	♣ Q 10 2	
♠ 8 7 2		♠ A 9 4 3
♡ K Q 9 3		♡ J 7
◇ J 2		◇ 9 7 6 4
♣ 9 7 6 4		♣ K 8 3
	♠ 6	
	♡ A 10 6 5 2	
	◇ A K Q 10	
	♣ A J 5	

South	*West*	*North*	*East*
1 ♡	No	1 ♠	No
2 ◇	No	2 ♠	No
2NT	No	3NT	End

West led ♣ 7 and declarer played the queen from dummy. Not giving the matter much thought, East covered with the king and declarer took the ace. It was now a simple matter for South to clear the spade suit and enter dummy with ♣ 10 to score twelve tricks.

East could read the opening lead with confidence. South's bidding left little room for a four-card club suit, so West's ♣ 7 had to be from ♣ 9 7 x x rather than a three-card holding such as ♣ A 9 7 or ♣ J 9 7. East should have held off his king at trick one, killing the quick entry to dummy's spades.

You may have noticed that declarer misplayed the hand himself. Had he played low from dummy at trick one and won in hand with the ace, dummy's ♣ Q 10 would subsequently have given him a certain entry to dummy's spade suit.

When you hold the ace in the suit partner leads, it is

sometimes a close decision whether or not to play it immediately. Take the East cards here:

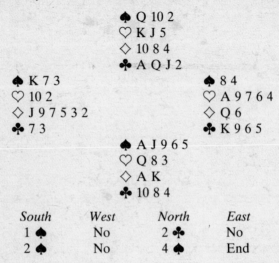

	Q 10 2	
	♡ K J 5	
	◇ 10 8 4	
	♣ A Q J 2	

♠ K 7 3   ♠ 8 4
♡ 10 2   ♡ A 9 7 6 4
◇ J 9 7 5 3 2   ◇ Q 6
♣ 7 3   ♣ K 9 6 5

                ♠ A J 9 6 5
                ♡ Q 8 3
                ◇ A K
                ♣ 10 8 4

South	*West*	*North*	*East*
1 ♠	No	2 ♣	No
2 ♠	No	4 ♠	End

West leads ♡ 10 against four spades and declarer puts up dummy's king. Since you hold ♡ 9, you can tell that partner's lead is either a singleton or a doubleton. Since declarer might well have rebid two hearts if he held four hearts, you should play partner for a doubleton in the suit. Even if no clue from the bidding presents itself, a 3–2 division of the missing hearts is mathematically more likely than 4–1. You should therefore duck the opening lead, signalling encouragement with ♡ 7.

Declarer takes an immediate trump finesse. Your partner wins and puts you in with the ace of hearts for a heart ruff. You cannot be denied your king of clubs, so the contract is one down.

One time to suspect a singleton lead is when the lead is in an unexpected suit. Say you have both been bidding spades, but your partner leads ◇ 9 against four hearts. Would he prefer a nondescript doubleton to a safe lead in spades? No, it's more likely that the lead is a singleton.

Declarer thought he had a difficult guess to make on this hand:

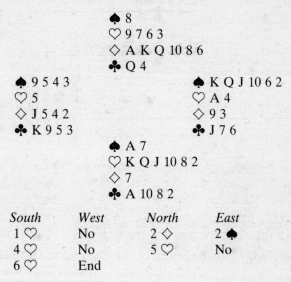

South	West	North	East
1 ♡	No	2 ◇	2 ♠
4 ♡	No	5 ♡	No
6 ♡	End		

West led ♣ 3 against six hearts and declarer had to guess whether or not to play dummy's queen. Reasoning that East had entered the bidding and was therefore more likely to hold the higher honour, declarer eventually misguessed, playing low from dummy. There was no way to retrieve the situation and the slam went one down.

Declarer had little excuse for misreading the lead. West would not spurn his partner's suit just to lead from a jack. It was much more likely that he had a high honour in the suit led and was hoping to establish a quick trick there.

QUIZ ON INFERENCES FROM THE OPENING LEAD

1.

           North
           ♠ A 7
           ♡ K 5 4
           ◇ A Q J 10 6 2
           ♣ A 10

                              East
                              ♠ Q 8 6 3
   ♡ 7 led   ♡ A J 10 2
                              ◇ K 3
                              ♣ 8 5 2

South	West	North	East
		1 ◇	No
1NT	No	3NT	End

Your partner leads ♡ 7 against 3NT.
(a) What heart holdings might he have?
(b) Declarer plays low from dummy. Plan the defence.

2.

           North
           ♠ K 10 8 4
           ♡ A 9 7 5 2
           ◇ Q 8
           ♣ J 7

                              East
                              ♠ J 3
   ◇ 3 led   ♡ 10 8 6 3
                              ◇ A 7 6 5 2
                              ♣ 5 3

South	West	North	East
1 ♣	No	1 ♡	No
3 ♣	No	3 ♠	No
3NT	End		

Partner leads ♢ 3 against 3NT and declarer plays dummy's queen.

(a) What do you think partner's diamond holding is?

(b) Plan the defence.

1.(a) 7 6 3, 9 7 6 3, 8 7 6 3, Q 9 7, Q 8 7, or Q 9 8 7.

(b) If declarer holds the queen of hearts, it's most unlikely that the contract can be beaten. He will have eight tricks on view after clearing the diamonds, with at least one black-suit king still to come.

If partner has led from Q x x and also holds the king of spades, you have a theoretical chance: win with ♡ 10 and lead back the spade *queen*, a Deschapelles Coup to create an entry to partner's hand.

But why should partner have led from Q x x? Surely that can't be his best suit outside diamonds. It is much more likely that he has ♡ Q 9 8 7. Your best shot at trick one is therefore ♡ 2, leaving partner on lead to continue the suit. Declarer may hold something like ♠ K J x ♡ x x ♢ x x x ♣ K x x x x.

2.(a) Partner cannot hold ♢ J x x, or declarer (with K 10 x) would have played low from dummy to ensure two tricks in the suit. Partner must therefore hold ♢ J x x x, ♢ K x x or ♢ K x x x.

(b) South's 3NT bid makes it most unlikely that your partner holds ♢ K x x x. At trick 1 you should let dummy's ♢ Q hold, signalling encouragement with ♢ 7. If partner has an entry in clubs (as you must hope), you will now be able to run the diamond suit. Playing the ace at trick one would block the suit if partner had led from ♢ K x x.

9

SIGNALLING

When partner makes the opening lead or switches to a new suit in the middle of the play, you will often have a chance to signal encouragement or discouragement. In time-honoured fashion you play a high card to encourage a continuation, a low card to discourage. In some situations, though, it will be more helpful to give your partner a count in the suit.

♣ A Q J

♣ 4 led   ♣ 9 7 6 2

Partner leads ♣ 4 against a major-suit game and declarer plays the queen from dummy. There is no point playing ♣ 2 to tell partner you don't think much of his lead. He can guess that! Signal with ♣ 7, showing an even number of cards in the suit. Tell him something that may be useful; at the very least it will help him to count the hand.

This is a common situation at notrumps:

♡ A K 4

♡ Q J 9 6 2   ♡ 8 7 3

♡ 10 5

Your partner leads ♡ Q, won in the dummy. When you signal with the 3, showing an odd number of cards, West knows that his jack will pin the 10. With a doubleton 8 3 in this position you would play high-low; with 10 x x, the 10.

Accurate signals can often undermine declarer's attempts to false-card:

♢ J 10 3

♢ A K 5 4   ♢ 9 7 6 2

♢ Q 8

Your partner leads ♢ A against a suit slam and declarer drops the queen from hand. If partner is unsure of the suit's distribution he may be unwilling to continue with ♢ K, setting up dummy's jack. You should give him a count on the suit by signalling with the 7.

There is one rather important situation in which defenders are sometimes in doubt as to which card to play:

♠ Q 9 5 3

♠ A K J 7 6 4   ♠ 8 2

♠ 10

Partner, who has bid spades, leads ♠ A against a high suit contract. You suspect, rightly, that declarer has a singleton in the suit. Don't play the 2, hoping to discourage partner from continuing the suit. If you do, he will be entitled to place you with a singleton. The correct card is the 8, showing your count in the suit.

It is sometimes important to give partner a count when declarer is playing on his own long suits. Defenders are often careless on this type of hand:

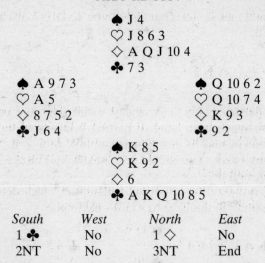

South	West	North	East
1 ♣	No	1 ◇	No
2NT	No	3NT	End

West leads ♠ 3 to the jack, queen and king, and declarer takes an immediate diamond finesse. If East holds off, with the intention of killing the diamond suit, declarer will cash the diamond ace and unveil his magnificent clubs, scoring nine tricks. West must help his partner by signalling his own diamond length. Playing the 5 would be a feeble effort (declarer might have led the 6 from ◇ 6 2); West should signal with the 8.

A peter in the trump suit carries a different meaning from one in a side suit. It indicates that you hold three trumps (or, very occasionally, five) and is especially useful when it tells partner that a third trump is held for a possible ruff.

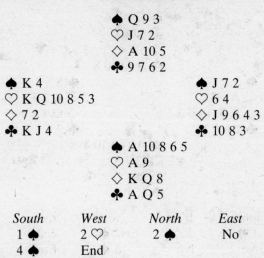

South	West	North	East
1 ♠	2 ♡	2 ♠	No
4 ♠	End		

West leads ♡ K to declarer's ace, East petering with his doubleton. Declarer plays ace and another trump, East following with the 7 and 2. West wins with the king and, knowing that his partner has three trumps, has no hesitation in cashing ♡ Q and playing a third heart. East's ♠ J is promoted and declarer must eventually lose a club trick for one down.

If East had followed upwards in trumps (showing a doubleton), West would have defended differently. He would have switched to clubs, hoping to set up tricks there before declarer could establish ♡ J for a discard.

When partner leads an ace against a suit contract, a signal of the queen indicates possession of the jack. It tells partner that he can safely underlead the king on the next round. Here is a typical use of the signal:

                        ♠ K 9 7 6
                        ♡ 10 8 2
                        ◇ 6 5
                        ♣ A Q 10 8
    ♠ 3   ♠ 8 5 2
    ♡ A 6 4   ♡ K J 9 3
    ◇ A K 10 9 3   ◇ Q J 8 2
    ♣ 9 6 5 3   ♣ 7 4
                        ♠ A Q J 10 4
                        ♡ Q 7 5
                        ◇ 7 4
                        ♣ K J 2

South	West	North	East
1 ♠	2 ◇	2 ♠	3 ◇
No	No	3 ♠	End

Partner leads ◇ A against three spades and you signal with
the queen. Partner crosses to your ◇ J and you must try to take
three heart tricks. Do you see how to do it? Lead the *jack* of
hearts and declarer is powerless. Such a return is indicated
when you have two intermediate cards which *surround*
dummy's highest card (here your ♡ J 9 surrounds dummy's
♡ 10 x).

There is another type of signal, known as suit preference,
which does not relate to strength or to length in the suit led; it
indicates your preference between the other two side suits. This
technique is especially useful when you are giving partner a ruff
and wish to indicate a route back to your hand. Take the West
cards on this deal:

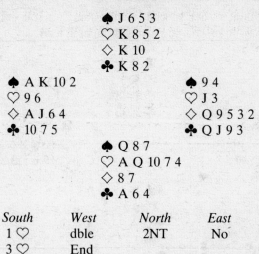

South	West	North	East
1 ♡	dble	2NT	No
3 ♡	End		

After a double, North's 2NT shows a sound raise to three hearts. Declarer signs off, expecting that the three level will be high enough. You lead your top spade honours and East shows his doubleton by playing high-low. You now have a choice of cards with which to give your partner a ruff. Since your re-entry is in diamonds, the *higher* of the other two side suits, you lead a *high* spade – the 10. East ruffs and returns a diamond, as requested. You can now lead a fourth round of spades, enabling partner to kill dummy's jack. Declarer has no way of avoiding a subsequent club loser and the contract goes one down. If your re-entry had been in clubs, the lower suit, you would have led ♠ 2 instead of ♠ 10 at trick 3.

In certain, rather special, circumstances a suit preference signal may be played on partner's opening lead.

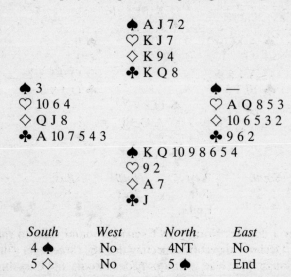

	♠ A J 7 2	
	♡ K J 7	
	♢ K 9 4	
	♣ K Q 8	

♠ 3		♠ —
♡ 10 6 4		♡ A Q 8 5 3
♢ Q J 8		♢ 10 6 5 3 2
♣ A 10 7 5 4 3		♣ 9 6 2

	♠ K Q 10 9 8 6 5 4	
	♡ 9 2	
	♢ A 7	
	♣ J	

South	*West*	*North*	*East*
4 ♠	No	4NT	No
5 ♢	No	5 ♠	End

The opponents climb dangerously high and your partner tries ♣ A as his opening shot. Dummy's club holding is not a pleasant sight; your partner must now find the right red suit switch. Help him by signalling with ♣ 9 on the opening lead. He will then switch to the higher of the other two suits – hearts. Note that without such an understanding West would probably switch to ♢ Q. In diamonds he needs to find you with only one good card – the ace – to produce two tricks. In hearts you will need the ace *and* the queen.

On this occasion it was obvious that you did not want partner to lead another club. Whenever there is *doubt*, play the normal type of signal – high to encourage. In other words, *don't play suit preference signals at trick one unless the position is very clear.* Sometimes you will be able to choose between *three* signals. For example, partner leads the ace of a suit where you hold K Q 10 8 6 3. Now play the 10 to encourage, the queen to ask for a switch to the higher-ranking side suit, the 3 to suggest the lower-ranking side suit.

QUIZ ON SIGNALLING

1.
                    North
                    ♢ J 8 4

                                East
    ♢ K led   ♢ A 7 2

Your partner (West) leads ♢ K against a major-suit game. Which card do you play?

2.
                    North
                    ♠ A K 8 2
                    ♡ 9 3
                    ♢ J 4 2
                    ♣ Q 9 6 3

                                East
                                ♠ Q 6 4
                                ♡ J 10 8 2
     ♣ A led   ♢ K Q 9 5
                                ♣ 7 2

South	*West*	*North*	*East*
1 ♡	No	1 ♠	No
3 ♡	No	4 ♡	End

Partner fires off ♣ A against four hearts. Which card do you play?

ANSWERS TO QUIZ

1. When partner's ♢ K wins the trick, it will not be difficult for him to place you with the ace. An encouraging signal in the suit would therefore be superfluous. Play ♢ 2 to tell him you have an odd number of cards.

2. Declarer must surely hold at least ♡ A K Q x x x and

◇ A. If you encourage a club continuation, you will have to ruff the third round with a natural trump trick and declarer will be left with ten top tricks. A better idea is to discourage a club continuation by playing ♣ 2 at trick 1. A diamond switch by partner has a good chance of establishing a fourth trick for the defence.

Part 2

FULL GALLOP

10

ELIMINATION PLAY

One of the commonest forms of end-play occurs in trump contracts, usually when declarer is blessed with plenty of trumps in both hands. The technique involved is known, rather sinisterly, as elimination play.

Declarer usually draws trumps first, eliminates one or more side suits from his hand and the dummy, then exits to one or other defender. Provided declarer has at least one trump remaining in each hand, the defender will not be able to lead back an eliminated suit without conceding a ruff-and-discard. He will therefore have to play another side suit, often to declarer's advantage. This is a typical example:

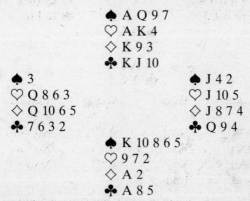

```
                    ♠ A Q 9 7
                    ♡ A K 4
                    ◇ K 9 3
                    ♣ K J 10
   ♠ 3                        ♠ J 4 2
   ♡ Q 8 6 3                  ♡ J 10 5
   ◇ Q 10 6 5                 ◇ J 8 7 4
   ♣ 7 6 3 2                  ♣ Q 9 4
                    ♠ K 10 8 6 5
                    ♡ 9 7 2
                    ◇ A 2
                    ♣ A 8 5
```

Playing in six spades, you win the diamond lead in hand. You draw trumps in three rounds, play ◇ K and ruff a diamond (eliminating the diamond suit). Next you play ace, king and another heart, eliminating hearts and exiting at the same time.

Whichever defender wins the trick will have an unenviable choice before him. A red-suit return will give you a ruff-and-discard; a club return will save you the club guess.

Look back at the whole hand again. Even if you held ♡ A K J, it would still be right to play hearts from the top. To take a losing heart finesse would cost the contract if you subsequently misguessed the clubs.

When you have a four-card side suit, you can sometimes exit on the fourth round, throwing a loser from the opposite hand. The defender put on lead may then have to give you a trick. Try six spades on this deal:

```
                    ♠ Q 10 7 2
                    ♡ A K 9 6
                    ◇ K 7
                    ♣ Q 7 5
      ♠ 8 6                        ♠ 3
      ♡ 3                          ♡ Q J 10 8 5 2
      ◇ 9 8 6 5 4 2                ◇ Q 10 3
      ♣ 10 9 4 3                   ♣ K J 8
                    ♠ A K J 9 5 4
                    ♡ 7 4
                    ◇ A J
                    ♣ A 6 2
```

South	West	North	East
			2 ♡
3 ♠	No	4 ♡	No
4NT	No	5 ♡	No
5NT	No	6 ♡	No
6 ♠	End		

East opens with a weak two bid, but you soar into six spades nevertheless. West leads his singleton heart, which you win in the dummy. You draw trumps in two rounds. What now?

You could eliminate the two red suits, then play ace and another club. That would succeed if West held ♣ K or if East held king doubleton (he would then have to give a ruff-and-discard). But remember East's opening bid; surely he will have the king of clubs. You should aim to end-play East with the fourth round of hearts. Cash dummy's remaining heart honour and ruff a heart. Two rounds of diamonds will leave you in dummy with these cards remaining:

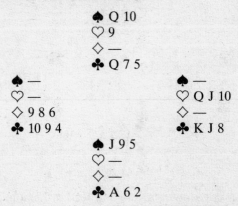

You lead ♡ 9, throwing a club from hand. East wins and has to lead from his ♣ K or give a ruff-and-discard.

Take the helm in six clubs on the next hand. West leads ♠ K. Can you see a way to improve on just taking two red-suit finesses?

If you can eliminate the spade suit you may be able to end-play East by playing a diamond to the 8. So, win the spade lead and ruff a spade. Cross twice in clubs to ruff two more spades and you are down to this position:

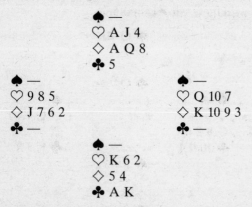

Now you cross your fingers and lead a diamond. If West follows with a low card, you play dummy's ♢ 8 and claim the contract. East is end-played and must give you a twelfth trick in one or other red suit.

Do you see how an alert West can put a stop to this? By inserting ♢ J he can prevent you from ducking the first diamond trick to East. Your only chance then would be to try ♢ Q. East would win and exit safely with ♢ 10, putting the slam one down.

Mind you, if East had been looking particularly smug, you might have tried a different line: ace, king and another heart, leaving him on play.

This hand showed one of the weapons you can use against elimination play – inserting a high card to prevent declarer from end-playing your partner. Another technique is to unblock high cards so that you cannot be thrown in.

Sitting West, you lead ♠ Q against South's four hearts. This proves to be a happy choice and you press on with two more rounds of the suit, declarer ruffing.

Declarer now cashes ♡ A K and leads a club to the king. You follow with your small club and . . . Do you? If you do, declarer will play ace and another club and you will have to lead away from your ♢ K or give a ruff-and-discard. To avoid this gory fate you must unblock ♣ Q under declarer's king. When he plays ♣ A you must continue the good work by unblocking ♣ J. Now your partner can win the third round of clubs. A diamond return from his side of the table will not give anything away. You will eventually score a hard-earned diamond trick to put the game one down.

Sometimes you may find that you have too few trumps, or not enough entries, for a neat elimination. Don't give up; as long as you can strip one of the defenders of his safe exit cards, your elimination may still succeed.

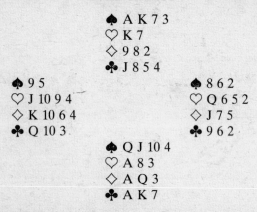

♠ A K 7 3
♥ K 7
♦ 9 8 2
♣ J 8 5 4

♠ 9 5
♥ J 10 9 4
♦ K 10 6 4
♣ Q 10 3

♠ 8 6 2
♥ Q 6 5 2
♦ J 7 5
♣ 9 6 2

♠ Q J 10 4
♥ A 8 3
♦ A Q 3
♣ A K 7

You reach one of your better six-spade contracts and West leads ♥ J. One ruff will eliminate the heart suit easily enough. But if you follow with three rounds of trumps, dummy will have none left. The ruff-and-discard element will be missing from any end-play.

The winning line is to eliminate hearts and take just two rounds of trumps, the ace and the queen. Then you play ace, king and another club, exiting to West's ♣ Q. Since he doesn't hold the outstanding trump he will have to give a ruff-and-discard or lead into your diamond tenace. This style of play is known as a *partial elimination*, since one of the suits – in this case, the trump suit – was not eliminated at the time of the end-play.

QUIZ ON ELIMINATION PLAY

1.   *West*   *East*
                ♠ A Q 10 7 3   ♠ K J 6 4
                ♡ Q 8   ♡ A 6
                ◇ J 4   ◇ A K 2
                ♣ A K Q 5   ♣ 10 7 6 3

South	*West*	*North*	*East*
			1NT
No	3 ♠	No	4 ◇
No	5 ♣	No	5 ♡
No	6 ♠	End	

You reach six spades and North leads ♡ 4. Plan the play.
(Trumps are 3–1.)

2.   *North*
                               ♠ 10 8 2
                               ♡ Q J 8 5 3
                               ◇ A J 3
                               ♣ A 6

        West
        ♠ K Q J 6
        ♡ 6 4
        ◇ K 10 4
        ♣ J 9 7 3

South	*West*	*North*	*East*
1 ♡	No	4 ♡	End

South wins your ♠ K lead and plays two top trumps, your
partner discarding a club on the second round. Declarer now
cashes ♣ A K and exits with a spade towards the 10. You
win ♠ J and cash ♠ Q successfully, everyone following. You
need two more tricks and you have ♠ 6 ◇ K 10 4 ♣ J 9
remaining. Which card do you play?

ANSWERS TO QUIZ

1. Normally you would let the heart lead run to the queen, but that would not be the best line on this hand. Win the first trick with ♡ A, draw trumps and eliminate the diamond suit. Now cash ♣ A K. Even if one defender holds ♣ J x x x, the contract is assured. You exit with a heart and whoever wins will be forced to lead away from ♣ J or concede a ruff-and-discard.

2. A club return will obviously concede a ruff-and-discard; if South had another club he would have ruffed it before exiting. You must therefore play a diamond – but which one? Consider this type of layout:

A J 3

K 10 4   Q 8 6 2

9 7 5

You see that the king is best? If you lead the 10, and this is covered by the jack and the queen, South will probably guess correctly on the next trick.

11

UNBLOCKING

In its simplest form, unblocking consists merely of playing cards in the right order. Every beginner learns at an early stage that when holding K x opposite A Q J x x he should start with the king. There is more to it than that, of course. How would you fare on this deal?

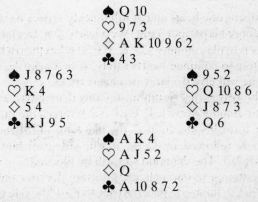

West leads ♠ 6 against your 3NT contract and dummy's 10 wins the first trick. Or does it? No, you must overtake in hand to preserve ♠ Q as an entry to the diamonds.

How should you continue? If you unblock ◇ Q and cross in spades to play dummy's diamond suit, you will be disappointed. The jack refuses to fall in three rounds and the contract goes one down. Do you see the winning play? You must overtake ◇ Q with ◇ A and continue diamonds until you force out the jack. As long as diamonds are no worse than 4–2, this play ensures five diamond tricks, more than enough for the contract.

Sometimes both sides have a chance to shine.

East opens one heart and South quickly arrives in 3NT. Not one to ignore his partner's suit, West leads ♡ 6. Declarer's best shot now is to play dummy's ♡ K. If East takes the trick, he will not be able to continue hearts safely. If he ducks the trick, of course, he will give declarer two heart tricks.

Say, however, that South misses this manoeuvre and plays low from dummy at trick 1. East's ♡ 9 forces the queen and declarer turns his attention to the diamond suit. If he simply plays ♢ K followed by ♢ A, it will not avail him to find diamonds 2–2. The diamond suit will be blocked.

In an attempt to untangle the position, declarer might lead ♢ 9 at trick 2, hoping to pass the trick to East, the safe hand. By giving up a diamond trick needlessly, declarer will remove the blockage and score five diamond tricks, enough for his contract. Mind you, an experienced player in the West seat might scupper this plan by covering ♢ 9 with the queen.

Requesting an unblock

Whether your style in notrump contracts is to lead the ace or king from combinations headed by A K, *reverse* your normal procedure in these two situations:

(a) When you decide to lead a short suit such as A K x, lead the ace (if your normal practice is the king).

(b) Equally, from a holding such as A K J 10 x or A K J x x x, when you want partner to play the queen if he has it, *reverse* your normal practice. The card you play, whether ace or king, conventionally asks partner to play the queen (if he holds it), to play the lowest from three small, and the higher card from a doubleton.

Imagine you are West on the following hand, defending 3NT.

> *North*
> ♠ A Q 5
> ♡ 9 4
> ◇ A Q 10 8
> ♣ J 9 7 2

> *West*
> ♠ 7 4
> ♡ A K J 8 5 2
> ◇ 9 3
> ♣ 8 5 3

South opens 1NT and North raises to 3NT. You lead ♡ A (your normal convention is the king) and await partner's card. If he plays the queen you will attempt to cash the heart suit from the top. If partner shows an odd number of hearts, by playing low at trick 1, you will continue with ♡ K, hoping to drop declarer's unguarded queen. Should partner indicate a doubleton heart, you must attempt to reach his hand by switching to another suit.

Unblocking discard

East was caught napping on the following hand:

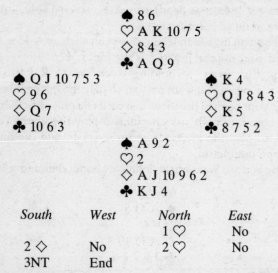

	♠ 8 6	
	♡ A K 10 7 5	
	◇ 8 4 3	
	♣ A Q 9	

♠ Q J 10 7 5 3		♠ K 4
♡ 9 6		♡ Q J 8 4 3
◇ Q 7		◇ K 5
♣ 10 6 3		♣ 8 7 5 2

	♠ A 9 2	
	♡ 2	
	◇ A J 10 9 6 2	
	♣ K J 4	

South	*West*	*North*	*East*
		1 ♡	No
2 ◇	No	2 ♡	No
3NT	End		

Missing the superior game in diamonds, South came to a halt in 3NT. West led ♠ Q and East correctly unblocked the king. Declarer ducked the first trick and decided, perhaps unwisely, to duck again when spades were continued. On the third round of spades East discarded one of his miserable clubs. Declarer won the trick, crossed to dummy with a club, and led a diamond. East was helpless. If he put up ◇ K, declarer would duck. If he followed with a low diamond instead, declarer would win with the ace and exit with a low diamond to the king. Either way the diamond trick would be lost to the safe hand, giving declarer his game with an overtrick.

The diamond king was an unwanted asset. On the third round of spades East should have dropped ◇ K like a hot potato. West's ◇ Q would then be promoted into an entry for the established spade winners. This type of discard – even the ace

when partner has Q x or J x x, or the queen when partner has
J x x – is often good play.

Unblocking to gain an entry

There are various positions in which declarer can conjure an
extra entry by unblocking a high card from the opposite hand.

$$\diamondsuit \text{ A 9 3}$$
$$\diamondsuit \text{ J 10 8 7} \qquad\qquad \diamondsuit \text{ K 6 2}$$
$$\diamondsuit \text{ Q 5 4}$$

West leads $\diamondsuit$ J and East's $\diamondsuit$ K wins the trick. By unblocking
the queen on this trick, declarer can ensure two entries to
dummy. It may seem good enough to play low at trick 1,
intending to gain a second entry by subsequently finessing
dummy's $\diamondsuit$ 9. West can thwart this play, though, by inserting
his $\diamondsuit$ 10.

Here is a similar position:

$$\clubsuit \text{ A 10 7 4}$$
$$\clubsuit \text{ Q 9 6 2} \qquad\qquad \clubsuit \text{ K 8 5}$$
$$\clubsuit \text{ J 3}$$

West leads $\clubsuit$ 2 to his partner's king. If entries to dummy are
scarce, it may suit declarer to unblock $\clubsuit$ J. The way is then
cleared for a finesse of dummy's 10.

QUIZ ON UNBLOCKING

1.   *North*
                           ♠ A K 7 2
                           ♡ 7 4
                           ◇ J 10 6 4
                           ♣ A Q 5

                                        East
                                        ♠ Q 10 3
         ♡ Q led   ♡ K 8 2
                                        ◇ 9 3 2
                                        ♣ J 10 4 2

South	*West*	*North*	*East*
1 ◇	No	1 ♠	No
1NT	No	3NT	End

Your partner (West) leads ♡ Q against 3NT. Which card do you play at trick 1?

2.   *North*
                           ♠ 8 5 2
                           ♡ 6
                           ◇ A Q J 9 6 2
                           ♣ K J 5

                                        East
                                        ♠ K 10 4 2
         ♡ A led   ♡ Q 9 7 2
                                        ◇ 5 3
                                        ♣ Q 9 7 2

South	*West*	*North*	*East*
1NT	No	3NT	End

Your partner (West) leads ♡ A against 3NT. (Your partnership agreement is to lead the king from a suit headed by A K.) Which card do you play at trick 1?

3.   *North*
                            ♠ 9 7 6 5
                            ♡ K Q 4
                            ◇ J 9 3
                            ♣ A Q 3

                                        East
                                        ♠ K 3
            ♠ Q led   ♡ J 9 6 2
                                        ◇ A 8 7
                                        ♣ 9 5 4 2

South	*West*	*North*	*East*
1NT	No	3NT	End

Your partner (West) leads ♠ Q against 3NT. Plan the defence.

ANSWERS TO QUIZ ON UNBLOCKING

1. If you unblock ♡ K at trick 1, you risk giving declarer a second heart stop when he holds A 10 x x or even A 10 x alone. Your partner will not be able to continue hearts if he gains the lead. Instead you should play ♡ 8, signalling your enthusiasm for partner's opening lead.

2. Partner's lead of the ace asks for an unblock, so you should play the queen at trick 1. He is leading from a holding such as A K J 10 x. It would not be good enough for you to 'signal encouragement' with the ♡ 9. Remember that in this situation a high card conventionally shows an even number of cards. Placing you with ♡ 9 x x x, partner would doubtless attempt to reach your hand by switching to a black suit.

3. Did you unblock ♠ K at trick 1? If so, you have just promoted declarer's ♠ 9 into a second stopper. Instead you should play low at trick 1. Let's say that declarer wins ♠ A immediately, crosses to dummy and leads a diamond. Now you must go in with ◇ A and unblock ♠ K. If partner has an entry in diamonds, he will be able to cash the established spades.

12

AVOIDANCE PLAY

There are many ways in which declarer may attempt to advance the play without allowing a particular defender (the danger hand) to gain the lead. The term *avoidance play* may be loosely applied to any such efforts. In the purest form of avoidance play the critical defender can gain the lead if he chooses to, but he has to pay too high a price for the privilege. Try 3NT on this deal. West leads ♡ J.

```
                    ♠ Q J 8
                    ♡ 8 4
                    ♢ A K 5
                    ♣ K 8 7 5 2
   ♠ 9 6 5 2                      ♠ A 7
   ♡ J 5                          ♡ K 10 9 6 2
   ♢ 10 6 4 2                     ♢ J 9 3
   ♣ 10 6 3                       ♣ A J 4
                    ♠ K 10 4 3
                    ♡ A Q 7 3
                    ♢ Q 8 7
                    ♣ Q 9
```

South	West	North	East
			1 ♡
No	No	dble	No
2NT	No	3NT	End

The bidding marks East with the heart length and both the black aces. Even so, you go through the motions of holding off the first heart and winning the second. What now? If you clear the spade suit, East will establish his hearts and you will be left with only eight tricks.

The winning play is to cross in diamonds at trick 3 and lead towards ♣ Q. If East beats air with his ace, you will have four club tricks. East will be on lead, but he will have paid too high a price for it. If, instead, East plays low, you will pocket your club trick and switch to spades at high speed.

The defenders will be just as keen to create entries to the danger hand as you are to prevent them. Unless you are careful they may be able to unblock high cards to good effect. How would you tackle 3NT on the next layout? West leads ♠ J.

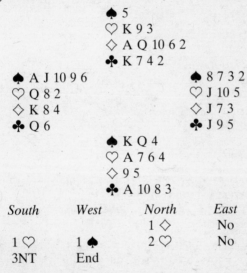

	♠ 5	
	♡ K 9 3	
	♢ A Q 10 6 2	
	♣ K 7 4 2	
♠ A J 10 9 6		♠ 8 7 3 2
♡ Q 8 2		♡ J 10 5
♢ K 8 4		♢ J 7 3
♣ Q 6		♣ J 9 5
	♠ K Q 4	
	♡ A 7 6 4	
	♢ 9 5	
	♣ A 10 8 3	

South	*West*	*North*	*East*
		1 ♢	No
1 ♡	1 ♠	2 ♡	No
3NT	End		

You win the spade lead and see that dummy's diamond suit offers the only real prospect of nine tricks. West is unlikely to hold ♢ K J x x so a double finesse in the suit is not the best line. Start with a low diamond to the queen. When this succeeds, it is important not to continue with ♢ A. If you do, West will gratefully unblock his king, establishing East's jack as an entry.

Instead, you should return to ♣ A and lead a second round of diamonds from hand. West is now powerless. If he plays ♢ K, you will duck. If he plays low, you will win with ♢ A and return a third round to his king.

When developing a suit, it is often right to finesse (perhaps unnecessarily) into the safe hand. This is the type of deal we have in mind:

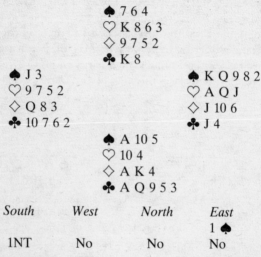

	♠ 7 6 4	
	♡ K 8 6 3	
	◇ 9 7 5 2	
	♣ K 8	

♠ J 3		♠ K Q 9 8 2
♡ 9 7 5 2		♡ A Q J
◇ Q 8 3		◇ J 10 6
♣ 10 7 6 2		♣ J 4

	♠ A 10 5	
	♡ 10 4	
	◇ A K 4	
	♣ A Q 9 5 3	

South	*West*	*North*	*East*
			1 ♠
1NT	No	No	No

West leads ♣ J against 1NT. East signals with ♣ 2 in the hope that West will find an inspired switch to hearts if ♣ J is allowed to hold. To prevent this, declarer wins the first trick with ♣ A.

Since only four club tricks are needed to make 1NT, declarer's next move is a low club to the 8, ducking the trick into the safe hand. This loses, as expected, but the contract is now safe. There is no entry to the West hand, so the defenders can take only four spades, a heart and a club.

Bearing the previous hands in mind, try this four-spade contract. West leads ♣ J.

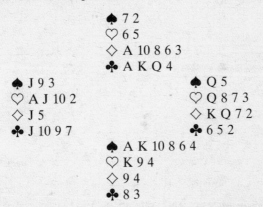

♠ 7 2
♡ 6 5
♢ A 10 8 6 3
♣ A K Q 4

♠ J 9 3   ♠ Q 5
♡ A J 10 2   ♡ Q 8 7 3
♢ J 5   ♢ K Q 7 2
♣ J 10 9 7   ♣ 6 5 2

♠ A K 10 8 6 4
♡ K 9 4
♢ 9 4
♣ 8 3

You win the club lead in dummy and lead a low heart, East playing low. There is no need to play ♡ K at this stage. You will have another opportunity later. Play ♡ 9 to keep East off lead. West wins and returns a trump to the queen and ace. Now you cross to dummy in clubs and lead another heart, putting up the king. West wins but cannot remove dummy's last trump without giving up his trump trick.

Look back and see what would have happened if you had played your ♡ K on the first round of hearts. West would win and play a trump. East would then take the second round of hearts with his queen and play another trump through your K 10. You would then lose three hearts and a trump.

QUIZ ON AVOIDANCE PLAY

1.   *West*   *East*
            ♠ A 10   ♠ J 7 3
            ♡ K J 3 2   ♡ Q 4
            ◇ J 9 5 4   ◇ A Q 10 8
            ♣ A J 5   ♣ K Q 7 4

You reach 3NT and North leads ♣ 8. Plan the play.

2.   *West*   *East*
            ♠ 5   ♠ A 9 3
            ♡ 8 5 2   ♡ K 7
            ◇ A 8 3   ◇ K 9 7 5 2
            ♣ K Q J 10 8 3   ♣ A 7 6

Bypassing an easy 3NT played by East, you arrive in five
clubs. North leads ♠ 6. Plan the play.

ANSWERS TO QUIZ

1. If you win the first trick in hand and take a losing diamond
finesse, South may put the contract at risk by attacking spades.
You should therefore play on hearts first. Win the lead in
dummy and lead ♡ 4. Even if South (the danger hand) holds
♡ A, you are safe. If he plays it on thin air, you will have three
heart tricks; if he holds off, you will switch to diamonds.

2. You could win the lead, draw two rounds of trumps with
♣ K Q and hope to establish the diamond suit without letting
North into the lead. On a good day you might be successful; but
there is a better way to play the hand. Play dummy's ♠ 9 at trick
1! Later you plan to play ♣ K Q, then ◇ A K and ♠ A,
discarding your last diamond. If all goes well you will ruff the
third round of diamonds high and enter dummy with ♣ A to
enjoy the two established diamonds.

13

KEEPING IN TOUCH

A declarer who has a suit such as A x x x x in dummy and x x x in hand will often duck the first two rounds. He saves dummy's high card until the suit has been established. Such plays are equally productive in defence. Take the West cards here:

```
                    ♠ 10 4
                    ♡ Q J 8 2
                    ◇ A Q 7 3
                    ♣ K 8 4
 ♠ A 9 8 6 2                        ♠ K 7 5
 ♡ 7 5                              ♡ A 9 6 4
 ◇ 9 5 4                            ◇ J 10 2
 ♣ Q 9 2                            ♣ J 6 3
                    ♠ Q J 3
                    ♡ K 10 3
                    ◇ K 8 6
                    ♣ A 10 7 5
```

South	West	North	East
1NT	No	2 ♣	No
2 ◇	No	2NT	No
3NT	End		

You lead ♠ 6 against 3NT. East wins the trick with the king and returns the 7, declarer playing the queen. To keep in touch with your partner you must duck the trick. Declarer has little option but to play on hearts. Your partner wins and crosses to your ♠ A. The run of the spade suit puts the contract one down.

If you are sitting West on this type of hand it is obviously essential for you to know how many spades declarer holds. If

declarer held only queen doubleton in spades, then holding off
the ace might prove disastrous. Your partner in the East seat
must give you a count on the key suit by returning the correct
spot card. From an original 3-card holding he returns the
middle card, as on the present hand. From a 4-card holding he
will return the fourth best, except when there is a danger that
the run of the suit may be blocked.

On the next hand East makes a similar hold-up, preserving
the entry to his long suit.

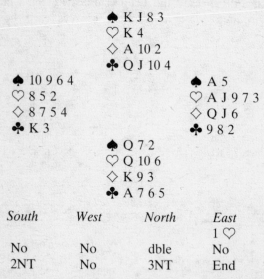

	♠ K J 8 3	
	♡ K 4	
	◇ A 10 2	
	♣ Q J 10 4	

♠ 10 9 6 4		♠ A 5
♡ 8 5 2		♡ A J 9 7 3
◇ 8 7 5 4		◇ Q J 6
♣ K 3		♣ 9 8 2

	♠ Q 7 2	
	♡ Q 10 6	
	◇ K 9 3	
	♣ A 7 6 5	

South	*West*	*North*	*East*
			1 ♡
No	No	dble	No
2NT	No	3NT	End

West leads ♡ 8 against 3NT and declarer sees that the
contract will be in danger only if West holds ♣ K. Hoping to
tempt East into taking his ace of hearts too early, declarer puts
up dummy's ♡ K at trick 1.

See what happens if East plays ♡ A immediately and returns
a heart. Declarer will win with the 10 and play on spades first
(attacking the entry to the danger hand). East can take the
spade ace and clear the heart suit, but West will have no hearts
remaining when he gains the lead with ♣ K.

East should, of course, content himself with ♡ 7 at trick 1, an encouraging signal. If declarer plays on spades, East will win and play yet another low heart. When the club finesse loses, West can cross to his partner's ♡ A and the contract goes one down.

On hands where the opening lead is from a doubleton, declarer can often succeed by means of a hold-up. Alert defenders can sometimes prevent the hold-up by accurate play in the third seat.

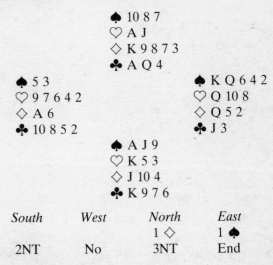

South	West	North	East
		1 ◇	1 ♠
2NT	No	3NT	End

Your partner leads ♠ 5 against 3NT. If you contribute an honour to this trick, South will hold up. A spade continuation will then be unproductive. Your partner will have no spades left when in with the diamond ace.

Instead, you should play ♠ 6 at trick 1, forcing declarer to take his second stopper in the suit immediately. When ◇ J is led, West will leap in with the ace and lead his second spade. Declarer will then be unable to establish the diamond suit without letting you in to cash your spade winners. The contract goes one down.

Note that if North had been the declarer in 3NT, you would automatically have led a low spade from the East hand rather than an honour, thereby keeping communications fluid. Your duck at trick 1 on the present layout was merely the same play from the other side of the table.

One type of communication play has an element of deception about it. Again the aim is to prevent a hold-up by declarer.

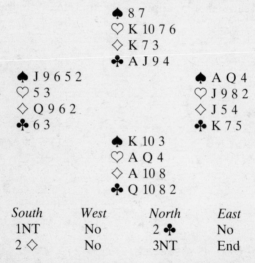

South	West	North	East
1NT	No	2 ♣	No
2 ♢	No	3NT	End

Imagine you are sitting East on this hand and your partner leads ♠ 5. If you make the 'normal' play of the ace followed by the queen, declarer will hold up until the third round. When he eventually takes a losing club finesse into your hand, you will have no spade to return.

See the difference if you play ♠ Q on the first trick. Declarer will not dare to hold up. He would look very foolish if the lead were from ♠ A J x x x and you proceeded to cash the whole suit. Having dislodged ♠ K at trick 1, you will be able to enjoy four tricks in the suit when you gain the lead with ♣ K.

Similarly, with ♠ A J x you should consider playing the jack on the first trick. This will force declarer's king when the lead is from ♠ Q x x x x. It is true that playing the jack would cost a trick if declarer held only ♠ Q x x, but unless he could run nine tricks immediately the contract would still go down.

We turn now to trump contracts. Here the defenders may need to hold up the ace in a side suit to obtain a ruff later. Take the East cards in this deal:

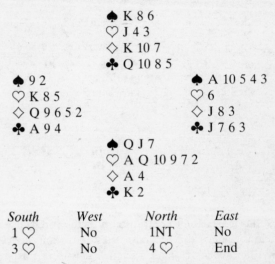

	♠ K 8 6	
	♡ J 4 3	
	◇ K 10 7	
	♣ Q 10 8 5	
♠ 9 2		♠ A 10 5 4 3
♡ K 8 5		♡ 6
◇ Q 9 6 5 2		◇ J 8 3
♣ A 9 4		♣ J 7 6 3
	♠ Q J 7	
	♡ A Q 10 9 7 2	
	◇ A 4	
	♣ K 2	

South	*West*	*North*	*East*
1 ♡	No	1NT	No
3 ♡	No	4 ♡	End

Your partner leads ♠ 9 against four hearts and declarer plays the king from dummy. You must decide now whether the lead is more likely to be a singleton or a doubleton. Since a doubleton is more likely, you will do best to hold off your ace, signalling with the 10. Declarer cannot now avoid defeat. When West takes his king of trumps he will cross to your ace of spades for a spade ruff.

On the next hand you must hold off the ace of trumps at trick 1 to stop declarer scoring any ruffs in the dummy.

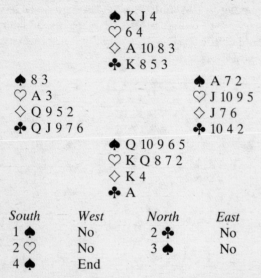

♠ K J 4
♡ 6 4
♢ A 10 8 3
♣ K 8 5 3

♠ 8 3   ♠ A 7 2
♡ A 3   ♡ J 10 9 5
♢ Q 9 5 2   ♢ J 7 6
♣ Q J 9 7 6   ♣ 10 4 2

♠ Q 10 9 6 5
♡ K Q 8 7 2
♢ K 4
♣ A

South	West	North	East
1 ♠	No	2 ♣	No
2 ♡	No	3 ♠	No
4 ♠	End		

West has no reason to fear dummy's club suit. Since there is an obvious danger that declarer may be ruffing hearts in the dummy, he decides to lead a trump. If, sitting East, you win with the ace and return a trump, declarer will play on hearts and eventually score a ruff in the suit. Your partner will have no trump to return when in with the ace of hearts.

The winning defence is for you to hold off the trump ace at trick 1. You will then be able to take a second and third round of trumps when your partner gains the lead in hearts.

QUIZ ON KEEPING IN TOUCH

1.

        North
        ♠ 9 4
        ♡ 10 5
        ♢ A Q J 9 8 2
        ♣ A J 3

West
♠ A 10 7 6 2
♡ J 8 3
♢ 6 5
♣ Q 7 2

South	*West*	*North*	*East*
1NT	No	3NT	End

You lead ♠ 6 against 3NT. Your partner wins the king and returns ♠ 3. Declarer plays ♠ Q at trick 2. Plan the defence.

2.

        North
        ♠ K 7 2
        ♡ A K 7 3
        ♢ Q 4
        ♣ J 10 4 2

                    East
                    ♠ A Q 9 6 5 4
♠ 8 led   ♡ 10 2
                    ♢ K 8 2
                    ♣ 9 3

South	*West*	*North*	*East*
1NT	No	2 ♣	2 ♠
No	No	3NT	End

Your partner leads ♠ 8 against 3NT and declarer plays low from dummy. Plan the defence.

3.

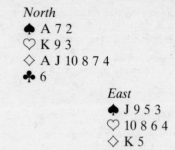

> North
> ♠ A 7 2
> ♡ K 9 3
> ◇ A J 10 8 7 4
> ♣ 6

♣ 4 led

East
♠ J 9 5 3
♡ 10 8 6 4
◇ K 5
♣ K J 2

South	West	North	East
1NT	No	3NT	End

Your partner leads ♣ 4 against 3NT. Plan the defence.

ANSWERS TO QUIZ

1. Partner's ♠ 3 return indicates that he holds either four spades or two. It would therefore be pointless to hold up your ace of spades. Win the second trick with the ace and return ♠ 2, hoping that partner has four cards in the suit.

2. It would be poor play to win with ♠ Q and clear the suit, hoping by some miracle to gain the lead with ◇ K. Instead you should hope that partner has a doubleton spade and a side entry – a club honour, perhaps. At trick 1 you should play ♠ 9 and hope for a happy ending.

3. Your best card at trick 1 is ♣ J. If declarer holds ♣ Q 10 8 x, he may take the queen, allowing you to run the club suit when you gain the lead in diamonds. If, instead, you play ♣ K at trick 1, declarer will duck your return of ♣ J. Communication with your partner will then be broken.

14

CROSSRUFFING

The golden rule when embarking on a crossruff is to cash your side-suit winners at the first opportunity. Otherwise the opponents may discard in those suits during your crossruff and be in a position to ruff your winners later. An example will make this clear.

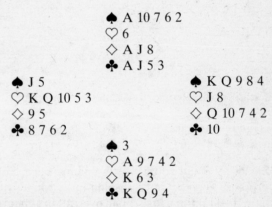

You play in five clubs and West finds the excellent lead of a trump. You win in hand, noting a promising route to eleven tricks – four side-suit winners, one trump trick already in the bag, and six further trump tricks on a crossruff.

You start with ♠ A and a low spade ruff; then ♡ A and a low heart ruff. When this passes by without mishap, you will need only two diamond tricks. What is more, they must be taken immediately. If you omit this vital step and continue with another spade ruff, West will discard a diamond and the game will be lost.

On most crossruff hands declarer has to risk ruffing with low trumps early in the play. On the next hand a different technique will prove safer. Look just at the North-South hands and the bidding and decide how you would play six spades on ♡ 5 lead.

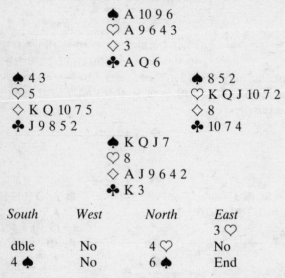

	♠ A 10 9 6	
	♡ A 9 6 4 3	
	◇ 3	
	♣ A Q 6	

♠ 4 3		♠ 8 5 2
♡ 5		♡ K Q J 10 7 2
◇ K Q 10 7 5		◇ 8
♣ J 9 8 5 2		♣ 10 7 4

	♠ K Q J 7	
	♡ 8	
	◇ A J 9 6 4 2	
	♣ K 3	

South	*West*	*North*	*East*
			3 ♡
dble	No	4 ♡	No
4 ♠	No	6 ♠	End

West leads ♡ 5 and you win with dummy's ace. Since you plan a crossruff, you begin by cashing three rounds of clubs. Now what? If you suffer a first-round overruff in either red suit, the defenders will doubtless return a trump, leaving you a trick short. The safe way home is to take three high diamond ruffs in dummy and three high heart ruffs in hand. A fifth round of diamonds will then ensure that you make either ♠ 6 or ♠ 7.

QUIZ ON CROSSRUFFING

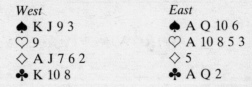

West	East
♠ K J 9 3	♠ A Q 10 6
♡ 9	♡ A 10 8 5 3
◇ A J 7 6 2	◇ 5
♣ K 10 8	♣ A Q 2

North leads ♡ K. Plan the play in . . .

(a) seven spades,

(b) six spades.

ANSWER TO QUIZ

(a)   In seven spades you must cash three rounds of clubs before embarking on a total crossruff.

(b)   In six spades it would be an unnecessary risk to play a third round of clubs. A defender might ruff the third round and return a trump. Take just two high clubs, then start the crossruff. In both contracts your first two ruffs will be with low trumps.

15

THROW-IN PLAY

In an earlier chapter we looked at elimination play, which occurs in a suit contract when a defender is forced to lead into a tenace or concede a ruff-and-discard. Other types of throw-in are possible but they often require accurate card reading. Sometimes the bidding will provide a clue to the opponents' distribution. Look at this hand:

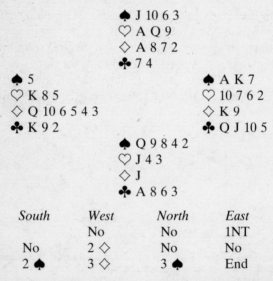

```
                    ♠ J 10 6 3
                    ♡ A Q 9
                    ◇ A 8 7 2
                    ♣ 7 4
  ♠ 5                              ♠ A K 7
  ♡ K 8 5                          ♡ 10 7 6 2
  ◇ Q 10 6 5 4 3                   ◇ K 9
  ♣ K 9 2                          ♣ Q J 10 5
                    ♠ Q 9 8 4 2
                    ♡ J 4 3
                    ◇ J
                    ♣ A 8 6 3
```

South	West	North	East
	No	No	1NT
No	2 ◇	No	No
2 ♠	3 ◇	3 ♠	End

After a spirited auction West leads ◇ 5 against three spades. You win in dummy and lead a club, allowing East's queen to hold. East plays three rounds of trumps with indecent haste and you see that you will now need three heart tricks to make the contract.

You win the third round of trumps in hand and lead ♡ J, covered by the king and ace. Next you ruff a diamond, cash ♣ A and ruff a club. When you return to hand with another diamond ruff, these cards remain:

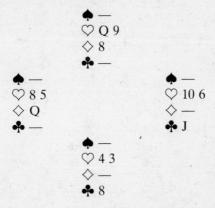

You exit with your last club, throwing the losing diamond from dummy. East has to lead back into the heart tenace and the contract is made.

Sometimes a defender finds he has to discard winners in order to keep a guard in one of declarer's suits. In the process he may lay himself open to an end-play. This next type of hand is quite common. Can you see a way to make 3NT?

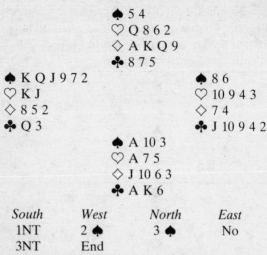

♠ 5 4
♥ Q 8 6 2
♦ A K Q 9
♣ 8 7 5

♠ K Q J 9 7 2
♥ K J
♦ 8 5 2
♣ Q 3

♠ 8 6
♥ 10 9 4 3
♦ 7 4
♣ J 10 9 4 2

♠ A 10 3
♥ A 7 5
♦ J 10 6 3
♣ A K 6

South	West	North	East
1NT	2♠	3♠	No
3NT	End		

West leads ♠ K and continues with ♠ Q when you duck. There's nothing to be gained by ducking again, so you win the second trick with the ace. It's important to preserve ♠ 10 as a possible exit card later in the play. Now you cash the diamonds, followed by the top clubs. This is the end position:

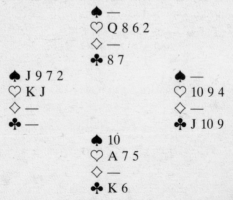

♠ —
♥ Q 8 6 2
♦ —
♣ 8 7

♠ J 9 7 2
♥ K J
♦ —
♣ —

♠ —
♥ 10 9 4
♦ —
♣ J 10 9

♠ 10
♥ A 7 5
♦ —
♣ K 6

On ♣ K West has to part with a spade winner to keep a guard on the hearts. It is now a simple matter to throw him in with a spade to lead from ♡ K.

On the next hand the actual throw-in costs you a trick, but the defender has to give you two tricks in return. Take the South cards and see if you would have spotted the play at the table.

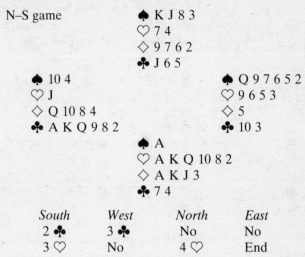

N–S game

    ♠ K J 8 3
    ♡ 7 4
    ◇ 9 7 6 2
    ♣ J 6 5

♠ 10 4   ♠ Q 9 7 6 5 2
♡ J   ♡ 9 6 5 3
◇ Q 10 8 4   ◇ 5
♣ A K Q 9 8 2 ♣ 10 3

    ♠ A
    ♡ A K Q 10 8 2
    ◇ A K J 3
    ♣ 7 4

South	West	North	East
2 ♣	3 ♣	No	No
3 ♡	No	4 ♡	End

West leads ♣ A and continues with two more rounds of the suit. You ruff the third round and play the ace of trumps, dropping West's jack. One more round of trumps confirms that West started with a singleton. What now?

The contract is in danger only if one defender holds ◇ Q 10 x x. If East holds ◇ Q 10 x x, you can make the contract by drawing trumps, cashing ♠ A and ◇ A and exiting with a low diamond. East would then have to lead into dummy's spade tenace or through your diamond tenace. But can East have four diamonds? That would leave West with a 5–1–1–6 distribution. Surely at favourable vulnerability he would have called three spades over three hearts.

Let's see what can be done if West holds four diamonds. The play must be to throw East in with a trump, forcing him to lead a spade. You draw a third round of trumps and cash ◇ A K. If East ruffs, he must lead into the spade tenace, giving you two diamond discards. If, instead, he discards on the second diamond, you will throw him in with ♡ 2. His fate will be the same.

Throw-in play is usually a less sure technique than elimination play, because the defender may create a guess by unguarding an honour card. That's what happened on this hand:

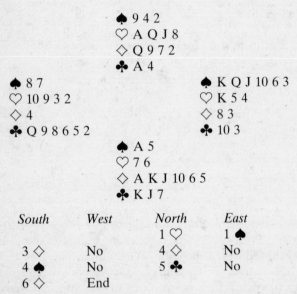

South	West	North	East
		1 ♡	1 ♠
3 ◇	No	4 ◇	No
4 ♠	No	5 ♣	No
6 ◇	End		

West led ♠ 8 against six diamonds, declarer winning with the ace. Trumps were drawn in two rounds and declarer ruffed his losing club. He then proceeded to run the trump suit, hoping to put East under pressure. East could visualize his fate if he kept ♠ K and ♡ K x as his last three cards. He therefore threw ♡ 4 and ♡ 5 at an early stage, followed by two intermediate spades. This was the ending:

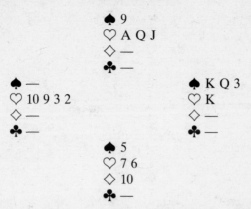

On the last diamond, East completed his deception by throwing ♠ Q. Put to a guess, declarer misread the situation and exited in spades. East's ♠ 3 became the setting trick.

QUIZ ON THROW-IN PLAY

1.   *North*
                                      ♠ A 8 6 3
                                      ♡ A Q 7 2
                                      ◇ A Q 6 5
                                      ♣ 9

                                      South
                                      ♠ K Q J 10
                                      ♡ 8 6 4
                                      ◇ K 7 2
                                      ♣ A 7 5

South	*West*	*North*	*East*
	3 ♣	dble	No
4 ♣	No	4 ◇	No
4 ♠	No	5 ♠	No
6 ♠	End		

Full marks for your enterprise in the bidding! How do you tackle the play on the lead of ♣ K? (East holds four trumps.)

2.

> **North**
> ♠ 7 3
> ♡ 8 3
> ◇ Q 10 7 5 3
> ♣ J 8 7 2
>
> **South**
> ♠ A K J
> ♡ A 10 4
> ◇ A J 4
> ♣ A K Q 5

South	West	North	East
2 ♣	No	2 ◇	No
3NT	End		

Game in a minor suit would have been more comfortable but you reach 3NT. West leads ♡ 5 to East's queen and you duck. Back comes ♡ 9. Plan the play.

ANSWERS TO QUIZ

1. Win the lead and ruff a club low. Return to a trump and ruff your last club high. Now draw trumps in four rounds, discarding two hearts from dummy. Then take two diamonds, finishing in hand. If West started with a singleton diamond, you cannot be certain of the endgame – a cunning East might come down to a singleton ♡ K and three diamonds. If East started with four diamonds, though, this will be the end position when you cross to dummy's ◇ Q:

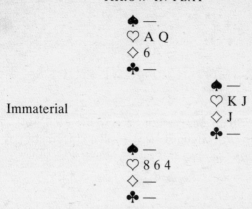

You exit with dummy's fourth diamond and make the contract whichever defender holds the king of hearts.

2. You should win the second round of hearts, planning to throw West in with ♡ 10. First you must extract West's clubs. If you make the mistake of playing three rounds of clubs you will be embarrassed for discards when West subsequently runs his hearts. You should therefore cash just the ace and king of clubs, hoping that West has a doubleton in the suit. On West's long hearts you will throw ♣ Q and a low diamond. This will be the ending with West on lead:

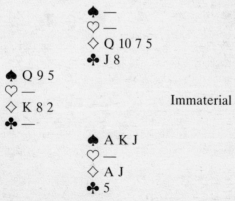

A ninth trick is on the way.

16

PROMOTING TRUMP TRICKS

When declarer fears an overruff he may choose to ruff with a high trump. In such circumstances it will not normally pay you to overruff. For example, this may be the trump suit:

```
                    ♠ 9 7 2
    ♠ A 10 3                      ♠ 4
                    ♠ K Q J 8 6 5
```

Your partner (East) leads a plain suit which declarer ruffs with the king. It is easy to see that overruffing would be wrong. If you discard, you are assured of two trump tricks.

On the following hand the position was a little less obvious and West did overruff – to his cost.

```
                    ♠ K J 7 2
                    ♡ K Q 10 5
                    ◇ Q 10 9 2
                    ♣ 5
    ♠ 10 9 5 4                     ♠ Q 8 3
    ♡ J 6 4 2                      ♡ 9 7 3
    ◇ 7 4                          ◇ A K J 8 3
    ♣ K 8 2                        ♣ A 9
                    ♠ A 6
                    ♡ A 8
                    ◇ 6 5
                    ♣ Q J 10 7 6 4 3
```

South	West	North	East
			1 ◇
2 ♣	No	2NT	No
3 ♣	End		

West led ◇ 7 to his partner's jack and East continued with ◇ A. When a third round of diamonds was played, declarer ruffed with ♣ Q and West overruffed. Declarer didn't mind this in the least. He won the spade switch with dummy's ♠ K and led ♣ 5. East did his best by rising with the ace and leading another diamond but it was to no avail. Declarer ruffed with the jack and drew the two remaining trumps with the ten, claiming nine tricks.

As in many situations of this sort, West should have refrained from overruffing. When declarer ruffed with ♣ Q he was, in effect, leading a round of trumps to which West *had no need to follow*. If West discards on the third trick, his partner will lead a fourth round of diamonds when in with the trump ace, promoting West's ♣ 8.

An attempted trump promotion will be ineffective if declarer can simply discard a loser instead of ruffing. Take the East cards on this hand and see how you would have fared.

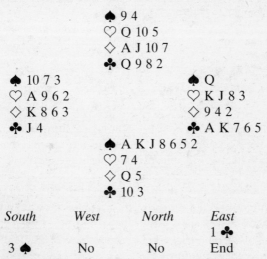

	♠ 9 4	
	♡ Q 10 5	
	◇ A J 10 7	
	♣ Q 9 8 2	
♠ 10 7 3		♠ Q
♡ A 9 6 2		♡ K J 8 3
◇ K 8 6 3		◇ 9 4 2
♣ J 4		♣ A K 7 6 5
	♠ A K J 8 6 5 2	
	♡ 7 4	
	◇ Q 5	
	♣ 10 3	

South	West	North	East
			1 ♣
3 ♠	No	No	End

West leads ♣ J, covered by the queen and your king. Imagine for the moment that you continue with ♣ A and another club. This will not be good enough. Declarer will simply discard a heart loser and now, even if West underleads his ♡ A and East plays a fourth club, South's ♠ J will hold the fort.

The most precise defence is to switch to ♡ 3 at trick 2. When West wins with the ace and returns ♡ 2 you judge that there are no more tricks to be made from hearts. You therefore cash ♣ A and try the effect of a third club.

This is a similar situation, more difficult to recognize:

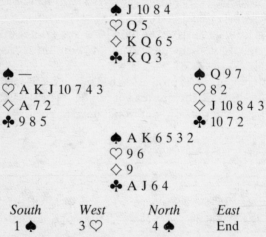

	♠ J 10 8 4	
	♡ Q 5	
	◇ K Q 6 5	
	♣ K Q 3	
♠ —		♠ Q 9 7
♡ A K J 10 7 4 3		♡ 8 2
◇ A 7 2		◇ J 10 8 4 3
♣ 9 8 5		♣ 10 7 2
	♠ A K 6 5 3 2	
	♡ 9 6	
	◇ 9	
	♣ A J 6 4	

South	West	North	East
1 ♠	3 ♡	4 ♠	End

West cashes ♡ A K, East echoing to show his doubleton. From West's point of view there is a fair chance that a third round of hearts will improve partner's prospects of a trump trick. Just in case declarer has only one diamond, West cashes ◇ A before leading a third heart. Declarer ruffs with dummy's ♠ J and the spotlight turns to East. He has no way of knowing whether declarer has another heart, but he can see that he is assured of a trump trick if he declines to overruff. The contract therefore goes one down.

Note how important it was for West to cash ◇ A when he did. Had West not done this, declarer would have discarded his singleton diamond at trick 3, losing just two hearts and a trump.

Now let's look at the situation from declarer's side of the table. Take the South cards here and try four spades on the lead of ♡ K.

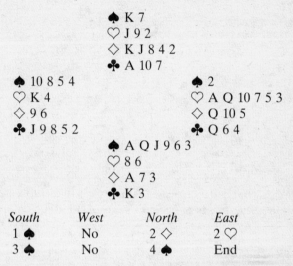

	♠ K 7	
	♡ J 9 2	
	◇ K J 8 4 2	
	♣ A 10 7	

♠ 10 8 5 4		♠ 2
♡ K 4		♡ A Q 10 7 5 3
◇ 9 6		◇ Q 10 5
♣ J 9 8 5 2		♣ Q 6 4

	♠ A Q J 9 6 3	
	♡ 8 6	
	◇ A 7 3	
	♣ K 3	

South	*West*	*North*	*East*
1 ♠	No	2 ◇	2 ♡
3 ♠	No	4 ♠	End

West's ♡ K holds the first trick and he continues with a second heart to the 10. East leads ♡ A at trick 3 and you must play from the South hand. Which card do you choose?

If you ruff, either with a high trump or the 9, you will go down. West will score a trump trick and East will eventually make ◇ Q. Instead of ruffing you should throw your possible loser in diamonds. Dummy can deal with a fourth round of hearts, so you will take the remaining tricks.

East's overcall of two hearts brought the risk of a trump promotion clearly into focus. Even without such a warning the diamond discard would still be correct play.

QUIZ ON TRUMP PROMOTION

1.

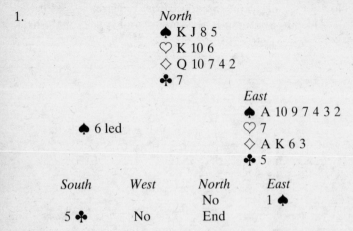

North
♠ K J 8 5
♡ K 10 6
♢ Q 10 7 4 2
♣ 7

East
♠ A 10 9 7 4 3 2
♡ 7
♢ A K 6 3
♣ 5

♠ 6 led

South	West	North	East
		No	1 ♠
5 ♣	No	End	

West, your partner, leads ♠ 6 against five clubs. You win with the ace, dropping declarer's queen. Plan the defence.

2.

North
♠ A J 8
♡ 9 8 6
♢ 10 9 4
♣ Q 8 5 3

West
♠ 9 7 6 5 3
♡ Q 3
♢ 8 7 6 2
♣ 9 4

South	West	North	East
1 ♡	No	1NT	2 ♣
2 ♢	No	2 ♡	No
4 ♡	End		

You lead ♣ 9 and partner wins with the jack. He continues with the ace and king of clubs, declarer ruffing the third round with the 10 of hearts. Plan the defence.

3.
                        North
                        ♠ Q J 3
                        ♡ Q 6
                        ◇ 10 9 6
                        ♣ K Q 10 7 4

                                    East
                                    ♠ K 10
            ♡ A led   ♡ 4
                                    ◇ K Q 8 7 2
                                    ♣ J 9 6 5 3

South	*West*	*North*	*East*
	3 ♡	No	No
3 ♠	No	4 ♠	End

West, your partner, cashes ♡ A K against four spades and
you discard ♣ 3 on the second round. He continues with ♡ 2
and declarer ruffs with dummy's ♠ Q. Plan the defence.

ANSWERS TO QUIZ

1. It would be premature to return a spade at trick 2. Even if
it did promote a trump trick in partner's hand, declarer might
well discard a singleton diamond and still make the contract.

The best card at trick 2 is ◇ K, on which partner will signal
his length in the suit. If he plays a low card, indicating three
diamonds and marking declarer with a singleton, you will
switch back to spades at trick 3 in the hope of a trump
promotion. If instead he shows a doubleton diamond you will
cash ◇ A and continue with a diamond or a spade, trying for
two down.

2. There is little chance of a spade trick in the face of
declarer's strong bidding. The best hope is to play for two trump
tricks by refusing to overruff at trick 3. If partner has ♡ K x x,
declarer is then likely to lose two trump tricks. Even if he places
you with honour doubleton and leads a low trump from hand, it
will do him no good. Your partner will win the trick with the

king and lead a fourth round of clubs to promote your ♡ Q.

3. This is no time to refuse to overruff! Partner had at least five hearts to choose from at trick 3. His play of ♡ 2 strongly suggests a club void. You should therefore overruff with ♠ K and return a club. A further point (in case it didn't occur to you) is that you are going to make only one trump trick anyway. It would be different if you held ♠ K 10 9 over dummy's ♠ Q J x.

17

REVERSING THE DUMMY

On most hands, taking a ruff in the short trump hand will gain a trick, whereas ruffing in the long trump hand will not. There is one type of hand, though, where you can conjure extra tricks by ruffing in the long trump hand, eventually drawing trumps with the shorter holding. Look at the North-South cards in the next deal and decide how you would tackle seven spades on the lead of ◇ K.

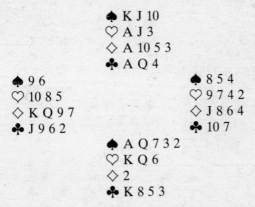

If you consider prospects from the South hand, the only possible loser is the fourth club. At first glance you may think that you need a 3–3 club break. You can improve on this slightly by drawing only two rounds of trumps before playing clubs. If clubs are 4–2 and the defender with the doubleton club has no trumps left, you will be able to ruff the fourth round of clubs in dummy. On the present layout this line will fail.

Try viewing the hand from the North position instead. There are three diamond losers there. Why not ruff them all in the

South hand, using North's K J 10 to draw the trumps? Win the diamond opening lead and cash the king and jack of trumps to check that the trump suit breaks 3–2. Then ruff a diamond low, cross to ♡ J, ruff a diamond high and return to ♣ A. Now you can ruff dummy's last diamond high and return to ♡ A to draw the last trump. You score seven side-suit winners, three trump tricks in the North hand, three ruffs in the South hand. Had two rounds of trumps revealed a 4–1 trump break, you would have had to switch to clubs, following the line described above.

On the next hand declarer wasted a slice of good fortune by misusing his entries to dummy.

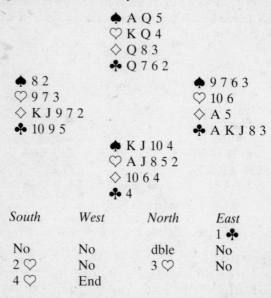

South	*West*	*North*	*East*
			1 ♣
No	No	dble	No
2 ♡	No	3 ♡	No
4 ♡	End		

West opened ♣ 10, which held the trick. A diamond switch would have proved fatal for declarer, but West continued with another club.

The stage was set for a dummy reversal. Declarer ruffed in hand, crossed to ♡ K and ruffed a third club low. He then crossed to ♠ A and ruffed dummy's last club with ♡ J. On this trick West seized the opportunity to discard his remaining spade. Declarer now cashed ♡ A and led a spade, trying to reach dummy to draw the last trump. West ruffed the trick and switched to ◇ J, putting the contract one down.

Declarer used his entries in the wrong order. Had he crossed twice in spades for the club ruffs, the dummy reversal would have succeeded.

There is a related type of hand where the declarer takes several ruffs in the long trump hand, merely with the aim of scoring his low trumps. On the next hand West leads ♣ 2 against four spades. Would you make the contract?

    ♠ 5 3
    ♡ A K 5
    ◇ A 6 3 2
    ♣ A 10 4 3

♠ Q J 9 4   ♠ 6
♡ J 7 2   ♡ Q 10 9 4 3
◇ Q 4   ◇ K J 9
♣ K J 6 2   ♣ Q 9 8 5

    ♠ A K 10 8 7 2
    ♡ 8 6
    ◇ 10 8 7 5
    ♣ 7

You win the ace of clubs and draw two rounds of trumps, revealing the 4–1 break. What now? Nothing! You're one down. At trick 2 you must ruff a club. Now you play two rounds of trumps, receiving the unwelcome news. You can still make the contract provided you can take one heart ruff and two further club ruffs in hand. Since dummy has three entries remaining, there is nothing to stop you doing this. You take four tricks in the side suits and six trump tricks.

QUIZ ON DUMMY REVERSAL

	West		East
	♠ A 8 7 2		♠ K 9
	♡ K 8 6 5 2		♡ A Q 4
	♢ K 7 3		♢ A 9 5
	♣ J		♣ A 9 7 6 4

South	West	North	East
			1 ♣
No	1 ♡	No	3 ♡
No	3 ♠	No	4 ♢
No	4 ♡	No	6 ♡
End			

You reach an adventurous small slam in hearts and North leads ♠ Q. Plan the play.

ANSWER TO QUIZ

There is no future in ruffing two spades since you will then lose a trump as well as a diamond. The best chance is to reverse the dummy, attempting to establish dummy's club suit.

Win the opening lead with ♠ A, cross to ♣ A and ruff a club. Take two rounds of trumps with the king and ace and ruff another club. Now back to ♠ K to lead a fourth round of clubs. If South doesn't follow to this trick, you are home. You ruff the club if he discards; you discard a diamond if he ruffs. Should South follow on the fourth round of clubs your best chance is to ruff, hoping that South holds the outstanding trump.

18

CREATING AND DESTROYING ENTRIES

When declarer's assets are equally divided between his own hand and the dummy, he is unlikely to have any problems with entries. For this reason a game with 13 points opposite 12 is usually a more promising proposition than one with 20 points opposite 5. When one hand (usually the dummy) is short of entries, many interesting skirmishes occur. Try 3NT here:

```
                    ♠ Q 8 5
                    ♡ 10 3
                    ◇ K Q 10 8 6 2
                    ♣ 5 4
    ♠ A J 7 6 2                    ♠ 9 3
    ♡ Q 8 4                        ♡ J 9 6 2
    ◇ 9 5                          ◇ A 7 4
    ♣ J 7 6                        ♣ Q 10 8 3
                    ♠ K 10 4
                    ♡ A K 7 5
                    ◇ J 3
                    ♣ A K 9 2
```

South	West	North	East
1 ♣	No	1 ◇	No
2NT	No	3NT	End

West leads ♠ 6 and East plays the 9. If you win with the 10 and attack diamonds, East will win the second round and return a spade. You will never reach dummy to enjoy the diamonds. If you play the king on the second round of spades, West will duck to prevent ♠ Q becoming an entry to dummy.

What could you have done about it? By winning the first trick with an unnecessarily high card – the king – you could have cleared the way to dummy's ♠ Q. The defenders would have no way to prevent you reaching the diamonds.

Sometimes you can conjure an extra entry by overtaking cards from the strong hand. Here is another 3NT contract:

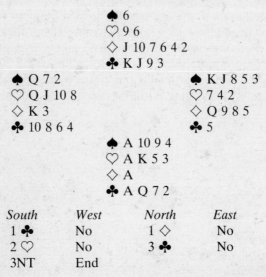

	♠ 6	
	♡ 9 6	
	◇ J 10 7 6 4 2	
	♣ K J 9 3	
♠ Q 7 2		♠ K J 8 5 3
♡ Q J 10 8		♡ 7 4 2
◇ K 3		◇ Q 9 8 5
♣ 10 8 6 4		♣ 5
	♠ A 10 9 4	
	♡ A K 5 3	
	◇ A	
	♣ A Q 7 2	

South	West	North	East
1 ♣	No	1 ◇	No
2 ♡	No	3 ♣	No
3NT	End		

West leads ♡ Q, which you capture in hand. You have eight tricks and only the diamond suit to turn to for a ninth. To make anything of the diamonds you will need three club entries to dummy. After unblocking the diamond ace, you cash ♣ A and lead ♣ Q. West follows, so it is safe to overtake with dummy's ♣ K. East shows out but that doesn't matter; you will be able to finesse ♣ 9 later.

Now, what about the diamonds? Which card should you lead? If they are 3–3, any card will be good enough. If they are 4–2 you must lead a low card, hoping that one defender has a doubleton honour. West wins your low diamond with the king. He continues with another heart, which you win in hand. Now you finesse ♣ 9 and establish your ninth trick by leading ◇ J from dummy.

Test yourself on one more 3NT contract:

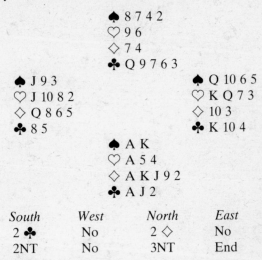

```
              ♠ 8 7 4 2
              ♡ 9 6
              ◇ 7 4
              ♣ Q 9 7 6 3
♠ J 9 3                        ♠ Q 10 6 5
♡ J 10 8 2                     ♡ K Q 7 3
◇ Q 8 6 5                      ◇ 10 3
♣ 8 5                          ♣ K 10 4
              ♠ A K
              ♡ A 5 4
              ◇ A K J 9 2
              ♣ A J 2
```

South	West	North	East
2 ♣	No	2 ◇	No
2NT	No	3NT	End

West leads ♡ J. East encourages with the 7 and you duck. West continues with the 10 and eventually you win the third round. What now?

Try leading ♣ J from hand. If East takes the king, you will be able to run the club suit when you regain the lead. If, as is probable, East holds off the club king, you will abandon the club suit and turn to the diamonds. When you cash ◇ A K the 10 falls. You can now drive out ◇ Q, scoring nine tricks. Note that the contract would have failed if you had cashed ♣ A before playing ♣ J. The defenders would then have had five tricks to take when you cleared the diamond suit.

When dummy contains two isolated winners, it may pay you to give up one trick to reach them. See if you would have made this four-spade contract:

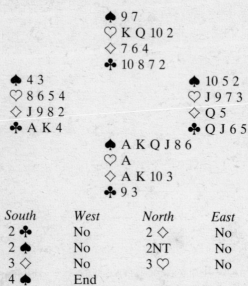

South	West	North	East
2 ♣	No	2 ♦	No
2 ♠	No	2NT	No
3 ♦	No	3 ♡	No
4 ♠	End		

The defenders begin with three rounds of clubs. If you ruff the third round with a low trump you can wave goodbye to the game. The diamonds don't break and if you try to ruff the fourth round East will overruff.

Instead, you should aim to reach dummy's heart honours by crossing in the trump suit. Ruff the third round of clubs with the ace, unblock ♡ A and lead ♠ 6 to dummy's ♠ 7. East will probably win and return his remaining club honour. You ruff high and cross to ♠ 9 to take two discards on dummy's heart honours. You lose just two clubs and a trump.

The defenders will obviously do what they can to prevent declarer establishing entries to the weak hand. Their principal weapon is the hold-up, as we have seen. Sometimes the defender in the second seat must make an unorthodox play.

This type of hand is common:

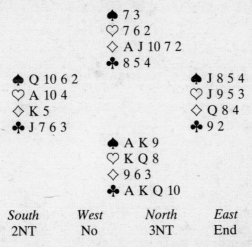

♠ 7 3
♡ 7 6 2
♢ A J 10 7 2
♣ 8 5 4

♠ Q 10 6 2   ♠ J 8 5 4
♡ A 10 4   ♡ J 9 5 3
♢ K 5   ♢ Q 8 4
♣ J 7 6 3   ♣ 9 2

♠ A K 9
♡ K Q 8
♢ 9 6 3
♣ A K Q 10

South	West	North	East
2NT	No	3NT	End

You lead ♠ 2 against 3NT, declarer heading partner's jack with the king. He now leads a diamond from hand. If you play low, declarer will finesse ♢ J and make the contract easily. It will make no difference if your partner holds off ♢ Q; declarer will simply continue with a low diamond to the 9.

See the difference it makes if you insert ♢ K at trick 2. If declarer wins with the ace, your partner will duck the next round, restricting declarer to one further diamond trick. If declarer decides to duck ♢ K, you will clear the spade suit.

Here is a similar theme:

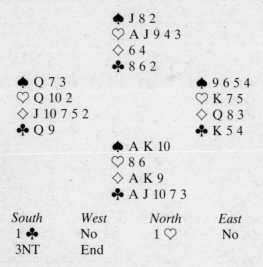

South	West	North	East
South	*West*	*North*	*East*
1 ♣	No	1 ♡	No
3NT	End		

You lead ◇ 5 to partner's queen. Declarer ducks and your partner returns ◇ 8, won by declarer's ace. Now ♡ 6 appears.

If you play low, declarer may try the 9 and partner will have to duck to kill the heart suit. Declarer will take advantage of this extra entry by finessing in clubs. Later he will cross to ♡ A for a second club finesse, scoring nine tricks.

To beat the contract you must put in ♡ Q on the first round. This will hold declarer to one heart trick and only one entry to dummy. It is true that if South had a high opinion of your defence he might try a different line – ♣ J from hand at trick 2. A right view on the next round would then win the contract easily.

When the next hand was played at rubber bridge, two mistakes were made. See if you can spot them as the play is described.

```
                        ♠ 7 5
                        ♡ A 2
                        ◇ A K 9 8 6 3
                        ♣ 10 6 5
♠ 10 8 3                                ♠ 6 4
♡ 9 7 5                                 ♡ K 10 8 6 4 3
◇ Q 10 5 4                              ◇ J
♣ K 9 2                                 ♣ Q 8 4 3
                        ♠ A K Q J 9 2
                        ♡ Q J
                        ◇ 7 2
                        ♣ A J 7
```

South	West	North	East
		1 ◇	No
2 ♠	No	3 ◇	No
3 ♠	No	4 ♡	No
6 ♠	End		

Thinking of this and that, East forgot to double North's heart cue bid. West led a trump – not an inspired choice – and declarer drew trumps in three rounds. He then played a diamond to the 9 and jack. Winning the club return with the ace, declarer crossed to ◇ A and ruffed the diamonds good. He was then able to return to dummy with ♡ A to take three discards on the diamond suit. The contract was made.

What were the two mistakes? When East won ◇ J he should have returned ♡ K, driving out the entry to dummy. This sacrificial play is known as the *Merrimac Coup*. However, declarer should not have given East the chance to shine in this way. He should have cashed ◇ A at trick 2, before drawing the remaining trumps. A second round of diamonds from hand would then have left West with no good answer.

QUIZ ON CREATING AND DESTROYING ENTRIES

1.
	West		East
	♠ K 8		♠ J 7 5
	♡ A K 6 2		♡ 8 5 4
	◇ A 10 9 7 4		◇ Q J 2
	♣ A K		♣ Q 10 6 4

South	West	North	East
	2NT	No	3NT
End			

After your somewhat dubious 2NT opening, North leads ♠ 4 to South's ace. South returns ♠ 6. Plan the play.

2.
	North
	♠ Q 8 5
	♡ A J 10 7
	◇ 9 7 2
	♣ J 8 3

West	
♠ 10 7 2	
♡ K 9 5	
◇ Q 10 6 5 4	
♣ 9 6	

South	West	North	East
1NT	No	2NT	No
3NT	No	No	No

You lead ◇ 5 against 3NT and partner's jack forces the ace. Declarer now leads a low heart. Plan the defence.

ANSWERS TO QUIZ

1. The key play is to unblock your ♠ K at trick 1. If the defenders persist with spades, the ♠ J will serve as an entry for a diamond finesse. If, instead, the defenders switch to hearts, you will unblock your club honours and lead a low diamond towards dummy. Unless the cards are very hostile, you will be able to score four diamonds, three clubs and two hearts.

2. It is quite possible that declarer has no entry to dummy outside the heart suit. You must therefore insert your ♡ K on the first round. If you play low, your partner will have to hold off his queen and declarer will be able to use the extra entry for a black-suit finesse.

Part 3

PAST THE POST

19

TRUMP CONTROL

Many hard-fought battles occur when declarer's trump holding is tenuous or when the outstanding trumps are breaking badly. To weaken declarer's trump holding, the defenders will often attack in their own strongest suit. By playing on this suit every time they gain the lead, they may be able to exhaust declarer's trumps, causing him to lose control of the hand. This type of defence is called a 'forcing game'. See how it works here:

```
                  ♠ Q 7 4
                  ♡ Q 9 3
                  ◇ A Q 5
                  ♣ K J 4 3
  ♠ A 9 6 3                      ♠ 5
  ♡ K 10 8 2                     ♡ A J 7 5
  ◇ J 7 4                        ◇ 10 9 6 3
  ♣ 10 2                         ♣ 9 8 6 5
                  ♠ K J 10 8 2
                  ♡ 6 4
                  ◇ K 8 2
                  ♣ A Q 7
```

South	West	North	East
		1NT	No
3 ♠	No	4 ♠	End

Sitting West with a promising four-card trump holding, you decide to play a forcing game. Hearts are your strongest suit, so you lead ♡ 2. This proves a great success. Partner wins with the jack and plays two more rounds of the suit, forcing South to ruff.

Declarer now plays a trump to the queen and a trump to the king. If you take your ace of trumps at this stage, the defence will be over. Declarer's minors are ironclad and if you play another heart he will be able to ruff in the dummy. Hold off for one more round of trumps and declarer will be a doomed man. If he persists with trumps, you will win and play a fourth round of hearts to remove his last trump. If, instead, he turns to the minor suits, you will ruff the third club.

It is easy to visualize a forcing defence when you hold four trumps yourself, not quite so easy when you hold a singleton trump. But sometimes partner is there with the four trumps and you must initiate a forcing game on his behalf. Look at this hand, for example:

West holds:

$$\spadesuit\ 4$$
$$\heartsuit\ K\ 10\ 7\ 6\ 3$$
$$\diamondsuit\ 9\ 8\ 7$$
$$\clubsuit\ Q\ 10\ 8\ 2$$

South	West	North	East
1 ♠	No	2 ♣	No
2 ♠	No	3 ♠	No
4 ♠	End		

You should attack declarer's trump holding by leading ♡ 6.

Declarer can often avert a dangerous force by arranging for the short trump hand to do any ruffing. Take the South cards here:

```
              ♠ A 7
              ♡ 9 8 5
              ◇ A Q 4 2
              ♣ K J 7 3
♠ 10 9 4 3                    ♠ K Q J 8 5 2
♡ A Q 6 2                     ♡ 4
◇ 7 3                         ◇ 10 8 5
♣ 9 6 5                       ♣ Q 10 2
              ♠ 6
              ♡ K J 10 7 3
              ◇ K J 9 6
              ♣ A 8 4
```

South	West	North	East
		1 ◇	1 ♠
2 ♡	2 ♠	3 ♡	No
4 ♡	End		

With a trump holding such as A Q x x, West knows what to do. He leads ♠ 10, attacking in the defenders' strongest suit. You win in dummy and run ♡ 9, losing to West's queen. Back comes another spade. What now?

If you ruff, West will duck the next round of trumps. You will then lose three trump tricks and a club whichever way you turn. Instead, you should discard a club on the second round of spades. Control of the hand is then assured. If the defenders persevere with spades, you will ruff in the dummy, preserving your own trump holding.

The next hand has a similar theme – using the reserve supply of trumps in the short hand to protect you against a force.

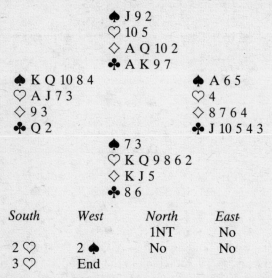

	♠ J 9 2	
	♡ 10 5	
	◇ A Q 10 2	
	♣ A K 9 7	

South	West	North	East
		1NT	No
2 ♡	2 ♠	No	No
3 ♡	End		

West leads ♠ K and the defenders continue with two more rounds of the suit. You ruff the third round. What now?

If you play ♡ K, West will duck. He will then be able to shorten your trumps twice more when he takes the ace and jack of trumps. You will lose control.

Since you can afford to lose two trump tricks, you should surrender one of them immediately. Lead a low trump from hand at trick 4 and West can do nothing. If he goes in with the jack, dummy's ♡ 10 will protect you against a fourth round of spades. And if he ducks, you will continue with a second round of trumps to the king and ace. West can force you once now, but you will cash the queen of trumps and run your minor-suit winners. West's master trump will be the fourth and final trick for his side.

Giving a ruff-and-discard is something that usually merits an apology to your partner, even a drink from the club bar. Not on

the following hand. Take the East cards and see if you would
have beaten the contract.

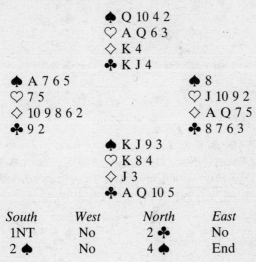

	♠ Q 10 4 2	
	♡ A Q 6 3	
	♢ K 4	
	♣ K J 4	
♠ A 7 6 5		♠ 8
♡ 7 5		♡ J 10 9 2
♢ 10 9 8 6 2		♢ A Q 7 5
♣ 9 2		♣ 8 7 6 3
	♠ K J 9 3	
	♡ K 8 4	
	♢ J 3	
	♣ A Q 10 5	

South	*West*	*North*	*East*
1NT	No	2 ♣	No
2 ♠	No	4 ♠	End

West leads ♢ 10 to your queen. When you cash the diamond
ace, declarer's jack appears. The two-spade Stayman response
denied four hearts, so declarer seems to have 4–3–2–4
distribution. How can you beat the contract?

Since your partner has four trumps, you should try to weaken
declarer's trump holding by giving him a ruff-and-discard. This
is unlikely to help declarer and will spell his downfall if partner
has the trump ace. Declarer will ruff in one hand or other and
attempt to draw trumps. West will hold off the trump ace for
two rounds and declarer will realize his fate. To avoid losing
control and going two down, he will have to abandon trumps
and attempt to run the clubs.

QUIZ ON TRUMP CONTROL

1.

	West		*East*
	♠ 6		♠ A 9 5 3
	♡ K Q 10 9		♡ J 7 4
	◊ A Q 8 5		◊ K 7 6 2
	♣ A K 9 4		♣ 8 5

South	*West*	*North*	*East*
	1 ♡	1 ♠	2 ♡
No	4 ♡	End	

North leads ♠ K against four hearts. You win with the ace and play a trump to the king and ace. North returns ♠ Q. Plan the play. Also, how would you play if the opponents declined to take either the first or second round of trumps?

2.

	West		*East*
	♠ A K J 10 7 3		♠ 6 4
	♡ 4		♡ K 8
	◊ K 8 2		◊ A 10 7 5 3
	♣ K J 5		♣ Q 10 8 6

South	*West*	*North*	*East*
	1 ♠	No	2 ◊
No	3 ♠	No	4 ♠
End			

North leads ♡ Q, which you cover in the dummy. South wins with the ace and plays a second round of hearts. Plan the play.

ANSWERS TO QUIZ

1. Discard a club on ♠ Q. If North persists with spades, discard a diamond. Dummy's ♡ J will now protect you against a fourth round of spades. If North makes a neutral exit, you will ruff a club high and draw trumps.

If neither opponent captured the first or second round of

trumps, the best continuation would be ♣ A K, ◇ A and a low diamond towards the dummy. If North discards and ◇ K wins, ruff a spade and lead a club. You will still succeed if North has, say, 6–4–1–2 distribution.

2. If one defender holds ♠ Q x x x you are in danger of losing control. You must take care to dislodge one of the enemy high cards (♠ Q and ♣ A) while dummy has a trump left. To play on clubs first might lead to a ruff, so best play is ♠ J at trick 2. If the defenders win and persist with hearts, you can ruff in the dummy.

20

THE PRINCIPLE OF RESTRICTED CHOICE

Understanding the Principle of Restricted Choice is something of a status symbol, even among experts. There is no good reason why this should be so. Despite its daunting title, the principle is concerned mainly with relatively simple finessing positions such as this:

♠ A J 10 7 3

♠ 9 6 4 2

You finesse ♠ J, losing to the queen (or king). When you lead a second round of spades from hand, West follows with a low card. Do you finesse again or play for the drop?

Most players know that a second finesse is the better play. Some might be surprised to hear that the odds in favour of the finesse are almost 2 to 1. Why is this so? Well, playing for the drop on the second round gains in only one situation – when East has ♠ K Q doubleton. It loses in two situations – when East started with a singleton ♠ K or singleton ♠ Q. Since these three situations are roughly as likely as each other, it follows that you will win two times out of three by taking a second finesse.

In the absence of special considerations, the best play in these finessing situations is expressed by the Principle of Restricted Choice: *It is more likely that a defender had no choice in his play of a card than that he selected it from two cards of equal rank.*

Let's see how this rule applies to some other familiar holdings.

$\heartsuit$ K 10 6 4 3

$\heartsuit$ A 8 7 2

You cash $\heartsuit$ A and East produces $\heartsuit$ J (or $\heartsuit$ Q). When you lead a second round, West follows with a small card. Do you finesse or play for the drop?

The rule says that it is more likely that East played $\heartsuit$ J (or $\heartsuit$ Q) because he had no choice (it was a singleton) than that he chose it from two equals (from Q J doubleton). You should therefore finesse on the second round.

Here is another situation of the same sort:

$\clubsuit$ K Q 9 2

$\clubsuit$ A 7 4

You play $\clubsuit$ K and $\clubsuit$ A, East following with $\clubsuit$ 10 (or $\clubsuit$ J) on the second round. When you lead a third round from hand, West follows with a low card. Do you finesse or not?

You finesse because it is more likely that East had to play the 10 from 10 x than that he *chose* to play the 10 from J 10 x.

Look now at a situation where restricted choice does NOT apply. This holding, for instance:

$\diamondsuit$ A Q 10 6 3

$\diamondsuit$ 8 5 4 2

You finesse $\diamondsuit$ Q, losing to the king. When you lead a second round from hand, West produces a low card. Do you finesse or not?

Restricted choice does not apply here since there is no question of $\diamondsuit$ K being played from two equal cards. In the absence of any distributional inferences, it is slightly better to play for the drop.

Even when restricted choice does apply, you must keep your eye on the deal as a whole. Try your luck with the South cards here:

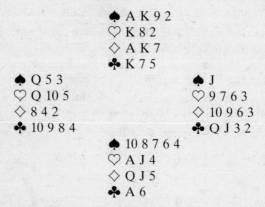

♠ A K 9 2
♡ K 8 2
♢ A K 7
♣ K 7 5

♠ Q 5 3   ♠ J
♡ Q 10 5   ♡ 9 7 6 3
♢ 8 4 2   ♢ 10 9 6 3
♣ 10 9 8 4   ♣ Q J 3 2

♠ 10 8 7 6 4
♡ A J 4
♢ Q J 5
♣ A 6

West leads ♣ 10 against six spades. You win in hand and cash ♠ A, East dropping the jack. What now?

Restricted choice suggests that you should finesse in the trump suit (which would indeed win the day), but there is a better play that is likely to succeed whether East holds ♠ J or ♠ Q J. Cash a second high trump. If East does show out, as on the present hand, you can eliminate the minor suits and exit to West's ♠ Q. He will have to give you a ruff-and-discard or lead a heart into your tenace.

QUIZ ON RESTRICTED CHOICE

1.   ♠ 7 5 2

                   ♠ K 10 9 4

You finesse ♠ 9, losing to the jack. Subsequently you lead towards ♠ K 10. Which card should you play and why?

2.

	West			East
	♠ K J 9 8 6			♠ A Q 7 4 2
	♡ 10 6 3			♡ K 7 4
	◇ A Q 7			◇ K 10 5
	♣ A J			♣ 8 4

South	West	North	East
	1 ♠	No	4 ♠

End

North leads ♣ K against four spades. You win in hand, draw trumps in two rounds, eliminate the diamonds and exit to North's ♣ Q. North now plays ♡ Q. How will you play the heart suit?

ANSWERS TO QUIZ

1. You should finesse ♠ 10. Think of it this way: With ♠ Q J x West might have won the first trick with ♠ Q. With ♠ A J x (or ♠ J x alone) he would have had no alternative. So play him for the jack, not the queen-jack.

2. Needing three tricks from the heart suit, any competent North will switch to an honour from J x x, Q x x or Q J x. Restricted choice tells us that it is against the odds that his queen was chosen from two equal cards – queen and jack. You should therefore play North for ♡ Q x x, covering the queen with the king. If South wins with the ace and returns a low heart, you will try ♡ 10. This play is a clear favourite since it wins also when North has led the queen from A Q x. (If you let the queen hold and North follows with a low card you will have a guess.)

21

FALSE-CARDING

Expert defenders are always on the look-out for situations where they may be able to mislead the declarer. There are many single-suit holdings where a well judged false card may present declarer with a losing option. This is a well-known one:

```
              ♠ A J 3
♠ Q 10 6                ♠ 8 7 4
              ♠ K 9 5 2
```

Declarer finesses ♠ J successfully and continues with the ace. If West plays a supine ♠ 10, declarer cannot possibly go wrong. Knowing that West holds the queen, he will play the king on the third round, scoring four tricks in the suit. Instead, West should play ♠ Q on the second round, *playing the card he is known to hold*. Declarer may conclude that East started with ♠ 10 x x x.

Some declarers allow themselves to be led astray on this holding:

```
              ◇ K J 9 7 3 2
◇ Q 5 4                ◇ 10 8
              ◇ A 6
```

The diamond ace is cashed and you drop the 10 from the East hand. Declarer may decide to play you for ◇ Q 10. This is a similar position:

```
              ♣ K J 9 6 5 2
♣ 10 8 3                ♣ Q 7
              ♣ A 4
```

On the second round you play the 10 from the West hand,

encouraging declarer to take the finesse. It is a mistake, though, to play these false cards on every occasion. If you do, declarer will be able to take advantage of many negative inferences. Here is a more advanced example:

♡ K Q 10 7

♡ J 8 6 3   ♡ 4

♡ A 9 5 2

Declarer plays dummy's ♡ K. If you follow with the ♡ 8 from the West hand, he may place you with the shortage and continue with ♡ Q from dummy.

On the next hand the defender in the East seat false-cards in the trump suit because he can see that declarer is bound to play the suit correctly otherwise.

♠ Q 10 9 3
♡ 6 4
♢ A Q 10 5 4
♣ Q 9

♠ 6   ♠ K J 7 2
♡ Q J 8 2   ♡ 10 9 5
♢ 9 7 6   ♢ 8 2
♣ A K 7 4 3   ♣ J 8 6 5

♠ A 8 5 4
♡ A K 7 3
♢ K J 3
♣ 10 2

South	West	North	East
1NT	No	2 ♣	No
2 ♡	No	3NT	No
4 ♠	End		

West cashes ♣ A K against four spades and switches to ♡ Q, won by declarer's ace. Declarer broaches the trump suit by leading low to the 9. It is clear to East that if he wins with the jack, declarer will finesse against the king on the next round. He therefore wins the first round of trumps deceptively with the king and returns a heart. Declarer wins and cashes the ace of trumps, finding to his surprise and annoyance that the game is now one down. You may think declarer should have played low to the 10 on the second round of trumps, allowing him to recover the situation when West shows out. But this play would lose if East had false-carded from K J x.

A lesser known but attractive position is this one:

```
                    ♠ Q 10 8
        ♠ 7 4                   ♠ K J 3
                    ♠ A 9 6 5 2
```

Declarer plays low to the 10 and you win with the king. On the next round he is likely to finesse the 8, losing two tricks in the suit.

Take the East cards on the next hand and see if you can lure declarer to his downfall.

```
                    ♠ Q 10 2
                    ♡ A J 6 5
                    ◇ K 5
                    ♣ Q J 7 2
      ♠ 8 7 6 3                    ♠ 9 5
      ♡ 2                          ♡ K 10 8 3
      ◇ J 9 6 4 3                  ◇ 10 7 2
      ♣ 9 8 5                      ♣ K 6 4 3
                    ♠ A K J 4
                    ♡ Q 9 7 4
                    ◇ A Q 8
                    ♣ A 10
```

South	West	North	East
2NT	No	3 ♣	No
3 ♡	No	6 ♡	End

West, your partner, leads ♠ 8 against six hearts. Declarer wins with the ace and leads a trump to the jack. What move do you make?

The layout of the trump suit is an open book to you. If you win with ♡ K, declarer will have no option but to play the ace next, picking up the rest of the suit. The club finesse will then see him home.

What will declarer do, though, if you play ♡ 8 on the first round of trumps instead of the king? Perhaps he will return to hand to lead ♡ Q, a play that would bring in the trump suit without loss if you held ♡ 10 8. As the cards lie, playing ♡ Q will prove a disastrous manoeuvre. You will collect two trump tricks.

Many opportunities arise when you have the lead against a notrump contract.

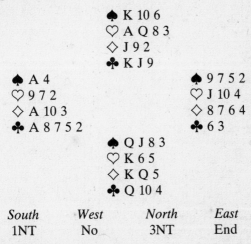

```
               ♠ K 10 6
               ♡ A Q 8 3
               ◇ J 9 2
               ♣ K J 9
♠ A 4                        ♠ 9 7 5 2
♡ 9 7 2                      ♡ J 10 4
◇ A 10 3                     ◇ 8 7 6 4
♣ A 8 7 5 2                  ♣ 6 3
               ♠ Q J 8 3
               ♡ K 6 5
               ◇ K Q 5
               ♣ Q 10 4
```

South	West	North	East
1NT	No	3NT	End

West is aware that he holds most of the defenders' assets. He therefore sees no harm in the deceptive lead of ♣ 2, pretending that he holds only four cards in the suit. Declarer wins and attacks spades. West takes his ace and leads another low club. Declarer can now count eight tricks – three spades, three hearts and two clubs. He marks time by cashing his spade winners, West discarding two diamonds. Declarer now has to decide whether to drive out the diamond ace or play for a 3–3 heart division. Testing the hearts and finding they were 4–2 would set up a fifth trick for the defenders. If declarer believes clubs are 4–3, he will probably try a low diamond from hand. West will pounce with his ace and surprise declarer by cashing three club tricks to put him one down.

This sort of trickery on the opening lead is most likely to prove effective when you hold the majority of the defensive high cards. Your partner's role in the defence will then be minimal, so there is little risk in misleading him.

A third-best lead from a four-card suit may be equally effective. The intention here is to convince the hapless declarer that you hold five cards in the suit.

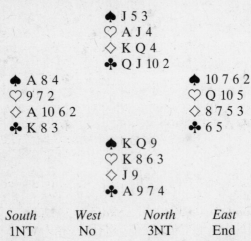

♠ J 5 3
♡ A J 4
◇ K Q 4
♣ Q J 10 2

♠ A 8 4
♡ 9 7 2
◇ A 10 6 2
♣ K 8 3

♠ 10 7 6 2
♡ Q 10 5
◇ 8 7 5 3
♣ 6 5

♠ K Q 9
♡ K 8 6 3
◇ J 9
♣ A 9 7 4

South	West	North	East
1NT	No	3NT	End

You lead ◇ 6 against 3NT and declarer wins in the dummy. Attacking the entry to the danger hand, he takes the club finesse. You win and return ◇ 2, maintaining the illusion that you started with five diamonds.

Declarer will scarcely dare play on spades in the face of this evidence. He will turn to the heart suit, hoping for a life-saving ♡ Q x x onside. Your partner will win the heart queen and the contract will go one down. Again, the fact that you held two aces and a king makes it unimportant that you might be misleading your partner.

When entries to dummy are scarce, you can sometimes persuade declarer to misuse them. Take the West cards again and try your luck on this hand:

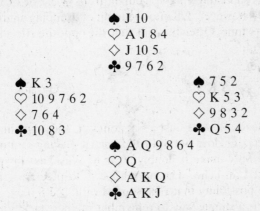

```
                    ♠ J 10
                    ♡ A J 8 4
                    ◇ J 10 5
                    ♣ 9 7 6 2
    ♠ K 3                          ♠ 7 5 2
    ♡ 10 9 7 6 2                   ♡ K 5 3
    ◇ 7 6 4                        ◇ 9 8 3 2
    ♣ 10 8 3                       ♣ Q 5 4
                    ♠ A Q 9 8 6 4
                    ♡ Q
                    ◇ A K Q
                    ♣ A K J
```

A long and learned auction leaves South in six spades. You lead ♡ 10 and declarer puts up dummy's ace, dropping the queen from hand. He then runs ♠ J to your king. Which card do you return?

Don't think too long about this, because your choice of return will make little difference. Declarer will cross to ♠ 10 and finesse successfully in clubs, making his contract. Your only chance of beating the slam, as you will have realized by now, was to duck on the first round of trumps. Declarer would then doubtless continue by running ♠ 10 and would never have a chance to take the club finesse.

So far we have been looking at false cards by the defenders, but declarer has just as many opportunities to deceive. The play on the first trick is often critical. Sometimes you will want to encourage a continuation of the opening lead, as here:

            ♣ 8 7 4

♣ A K 10 3   ♣ J 9 5

            ♣ Q 6 2

West leads ♣ A against a suit contract and East follows with the 5. If you drop the 6 from hand, West may conclude that his partner is signalling encouragement from ♣ 5 2 or ♣ Q 5 2.

Do not, however, fall into the habit of dropping an irregular card every time. Often this will have the opposite effect to what you intend.

            ◇ 10 7 2

◇ A K 9 3   ◇ Q 6 5

            ◇ J 8 4

West leads ◇ A against a suit contract, East signalling with ◇ 6. Declarer does not aid his cause by playing ◇ J or ◇ 8. This will only make it doubly clear to West that his partner has started an echo. The only hope is to play ◇ 4, leaving open the possibility that East started with ◇ J 8 6.

There is a simple way to remember the best tactics in these situations. Play a high card when you want a continuation and a low card otherwise – just the same as you would if defending in the East seat.

When the defenders are threatening a ruff, desperate measures may be needed. Take the South hand here and see if you can think quickly enough.

```
              ♠ K 9
              ♡ A 8 7 2
              ◇ A K 7 6
              ♣ J 9 7
♠ 7 5 4 2                        ♠ 6
♡ 9 6 3                          ♡ Q J 10
◇ J 10 5 4 2                     ◇ 9 3
♣ 5                             ♣ A Q 10 8 6 4 3
              ♠ A Q J 10 8 3
              ♡ K 5 4
              ◇ Q 8
              ♣ K 2
```

South	West	North	East
			3 ♣
3 ♠	No	4 ◇	No
4 ♠	No	5 ♠	No
6 ♠	End		

You reach six spades (instead of 6NT) and West leads ♣ 5 to
the ace. What is your reaction?

Don't start thinking of a plan yet. Drop ♣ K on the first trick
as naturally as possible! The first priority is to avert the club
ruff. There will be plenty of time later to sit back and see if any
route to twelve tricks presents itself.

Let's suppose that East falls for your deception and switches
to a heart. You win in dummy and run the trump suit, hoping to
cause the defenders some problems. This is the position when
you lead your last trump.

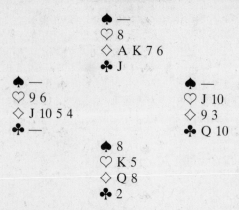

West has to discard a heart on your last trump; North and East both throw clubs. Now when you play the three high diamonds East will have to unguard the clubs or the hearts, giving you a twelfth trick. So, your false card at trick 1 is rewarded. There was no need to foresee such an end position – only to realize that following with ♣ K was the only hope.

QUIZ ON FALSE-CARDING

1.

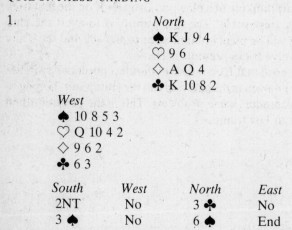

You lead ♡ 2 against six spades and your partner's ♡ J forces declarer's king. Declarer leads ♠ 2 from hand. Which card do you play, and why?

2.   *North*
                           ♠ 9
                           ♡ A Q J
                           ♢ Q J 10 4
                           ♣ K J 10 7 3
                                          East
                                          ♠ 7 6 4
                                          ♡ 9 8 6 2
                                          ♢ K 7 3
                                          ♣ A Q 4

South	*West*	*North*	*East*
		1 ♣	No
1 ♢	1 ♠	2 ♢	2 ♠
2NT	No	3NT	End

Your partner leads ♠ K against 3NT and continues with ♠ Q and ♠ J, declarer winning the third round. Declarer now leads a club to the jack. Plan the defence.

ANSWERS TO QUIZ ON FALSE-CARDING

1. You should play ♠ 8 on the first round of trumps, in case your partner has the singleton ace. This will then present declarer with a losing option in the suit. If he believes that your partner started with ♠ A 10 5 3, he will play dummy's remaining trump honour on the second round. Even if he leads from his Q 7 x towards dummy's K 9 x and sees you produce a low card, it will be a brave man who finesses the 9 on the second round!

2. You should win ♣ J with the ace and switch to ♢ 7. If declarer places ♣ Q onside, he will be able to count nine tricks – four clubs, three hearts, a diamond and a spade. He will therefore rise with ♢ A and repeat the club finesse. Trying hard not to smirk, you will win with ♣ Q and cash ♢ K to put declarer one down.

22

TRUMP REDUCTION

When you hold A Q of trumps and the defender to your right has K x, you may be able to perform a finesse even though dummy has no trumps remaining. If you can arrange to lead a plain suit from dummy at trick 12, you will prevent the defender's king taking a trick. That is just what happened on this hand:

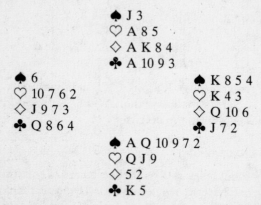

West led ♡ 2 against six spades and East's king won the first trick. A heart was returned and declarer won in dummy to run ♠ J. This manoeuvre succeeded, but when he continued with a spade to the 10, West discarded.

Declarer now had to aim for the ending where he would have just ♠ A Q remaining and the lead would be in dummy. He cashed his last heart, played two rounds of clubs and ruffed a club. He then crossed to ♢ A and led another club. East could only discard a diamond and declarer ruffed for the second time, reducing his trumps to just ♠ A Q.

Finally he crossed to ◇ K and gazed admiringly at this end position:

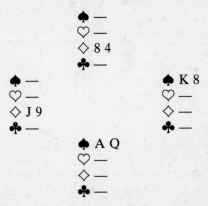

By leading a plain card from dummy the declarer was able to finesse against East's king of trumps. This technique is known as a *trump coup*. Note how important it was for declarer to reduce his trumps to the same length as East's. If he had omitted to do this and come to an ending with, say, ◇ 8 4 ♣ 9 opposite ♠ A Q 9, he would have had to ruff at trick 11 and lead away from ♠ A Q.

On the next hand you reach seven hearts and West leads ♣ K.

♠ K 10 8 5
♡ 5
◇ A Q J 3
♣ A 10 7 6

♠ J 7 3
♡ 4
◇ 9 8 6 2
♣ K Q J 4 2

♠ Q 9 2
♡ J 9 7 2
◇ 10 7 4
♣ 9 5 3

♠ A 6 4
♡ A K Q 10 8 6 3
◇ K 5
♣ 8

You win the club lead in dummy and pause for thought. You have no intention of finessing in trumps, of course, but you may have to prepare for a trump coup, just in case East turns up with ♡ J x x x. You would then need to ruff three clubs and still be able to return to dummy for the plain-suit lead through East. Because of the entry situation you must take the first of those ruffs now.

You ruff a club at trick 2 and cash two rounds of trumps, West showing out on the second round. Now your foresight will be rewarded. You cross to ◇ J and ruff a second club. Then you return to dummy by overtaking the diamond king.

Another vital stage in the hand has been reached. You must now cash ◇ Q before leading a fourth club. If you do not, East will beat you by discarding his last diamond on the club. You play ◇ Q and ruff the fourth club. You then play ♠ A, ♠ K and turn modestly towards East. The lead is in dummy and you hold ♡ Q 10 over his ♡ J 9.

These tidy trump coups are less frequent than the type known as *coup en passant*, where you promote a bare trump honour by leading a plain card towards it. Here is a straightforward example:

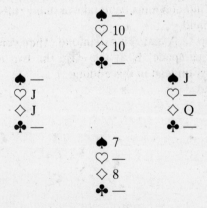

♠ K 8
♡ 10 9 7 6
◇ A 10 3 2
♣ A 6 4

♠ 10 6 5   ♠ J 9 4 3
♡ J 8 5 2   ♡ 3
◇ J 7 4   ◇ Q 9 5
♣ Q J 9   ♣ 8 7 5 3 2

♠ A Q 7 2
♡ A K Q 4
◇ K 8 6
♣ K 10

South	West	North	East
2NT	No	3 ♣	No
3 ♡	No	5 ♡	No
6 ♡	End		

West opens ♣ Q against your heart slam. You win with the king and play two rounds of trumps, discovering a loser in that suit. It seems you must also lose a diamond trick, but see what happens when you cash your top winners and ruff a club in hand. This will be the end position:

♠ —
♡ 10
◇ 10
♣ —

♠ —   ♠ J
♡ J   ♡ —
◇ J   ◇ Q
♣ —   ♣ —

♠ 7
♡ —
◇ 8
♣ —

A spade lead now promotes dummy's ♡ 10. The defenders' two tricks have been elided into one.

When the defender in front of you has a sequence of trump honours, he may find he has to ruff high at some stage to prevent your scoring a low trump. Provided you discard on this trick, rather than overruffing, your trump holding will move up a notch. The next deal is a spectacular example of the play.

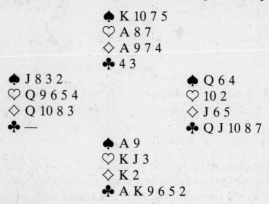

```
              ♠ K 10 7 5
              ♡ A 8 7
              ♢ A 9 7 4
              ♣ 4 3
♠ J 8 3 2                    ♠ Q 6 4
♡ Q 9 6 5 4                  ♡ 10 2
♢ Q 10 8 3                   ♢ J 6 5
♣ —                          ♣ Q J 10 8 7
              ♠ A 9
              ♡ K J 3
              ♢ K 2
              ♣ A K 9 6 5 2
```

West leads ♢ 3 against five clubs and you win with ♢ K. When West shows out on ♣ A, the hand suddenly becomes interesting. Your aim must be to take as many ruffs as possible in your own hand.

You cross to ♢ A and ruff a diamond. Then you play ♠ A, ♠ K and ruff a spade. Next you cash the two high hearts, leaving dummy on lead in this ending:

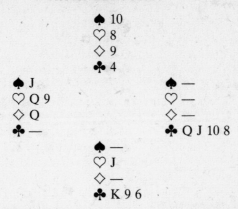

You don't lead a trump, of course; a plain-suit lead is much more powerful. When you play a spade East has to trump with the queen to prevent you scoring ♣ 9. You discard your heart loser, noting that your ♣ K 9 6 is looking considerably more robust than it did a trick ago. East leads ♣ J and you underplay this with ♣ 6. With a resigned air East leads from his ♣ 10 8 into your ♣ K 9.

We can now look at the other side of the coin – defending against trump coups. Many such coups succeed because the defenders persist in forcing declarer, thereby assisting him to reduce his trump length. Imagine you have doubled declarer in four hearts and you hold ♠ x x ♡ Q 10 8 x ◇ A K Q x ♣ x x x. Lead the diamond ace by all means and take what tricks you can in the suit, but then switch elsewhere. If you continue to punch declarer in diamonds, he will score his low trumps and maybe edge nearer to a trump coup in the endgame.

See the difference between good defence and bad on this hand:

```
              ♠ 5
              ♡ K 7 6 4
              ◇ A 10 7 6
              ♣ K 8 6 3
♠ K 10 8 7                      ♠ J
♡ Q J 10 2                      ♡ A 9 8 3
◇ J 5 2                         ◇ Q 9 4 3
♣ Q 7                           ♣ J 10 9 4
              ♠ A Q 9 6 4 3 2
              ♡ 5
              ◇ K 8
              ♣ A 5 2
```

South	West	North	East
1 ♠	No	2 ♣	No
3 ♠	No	3NT	No
4 ♠	End		

West led ♡ Q against four spades. Declarer ducked in dummy and East signalled with ♡ 9 to indicate an even number of cards in the suit. When West continued with ♡ J, declarer ruffed and crossed to ♣ K for a trump finesse. This lost to the king and West, most unadvisedly, continued with yet another heart.

Declarer ruffed in hand, cashed ♣ A and played three rounds of diamonds, ruffing the third round in hand. Thanks to generous co-operation from the defenders, declarer's trump length was now the same as West's. This was the end position:

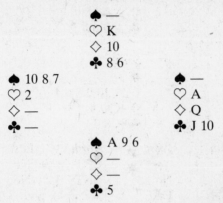

Declarer now exited in clubs, West discarding his heart. When East returned a club, declarer ruffed with ♠ 6 and West overruffed with ♠ 7. Declarer faced his A 9 tenace in trumps and claimed the contract.

Declarer could not have achieved this end position under his own steam. If the defenders had played on the minor suits instead of persisting with hearts, declarer would have had no chance to reduce his trump length to match West's.

QUIZ ON TRUMP REDUCTION

1.

> **North**
> ♠ A K Q J
> ♡ J 2
> ◇ A J 5
> ♣ A 9 6 4

♠ 10 led

> **South**
> ♠ 3
> ♡ A 10 9 8 6 4
> ◇ K Q 4
> ♣ K 8 3

South	West	North	East
		2NT	No
3 ♡	No	3NT	No
6 ♡	End		

Does the bidding strike you as . . . what shall we say . . . provincial? We wouldn't disagree. Anyhow, West leads ♠ 10 against your six-heart contract. Plan the play.

2.

       North
       ♠ K Q
       ♡ 8 3
       ◇ K 8 7 4
       ♣ A Q J 10 5

 ◇ Q led

       South
       ♠ A 9 3
       ♡ A K J 10 7 6 2
       ◇ 3
       ♣ K 3

South	West	North	East
		1 ♣	No
2 ♡	No	3 ♣	No
3 ♡	No	4 ♡	No
4NT	No	5 ◇	No
6 ♡	End		

West leads ◇ Q against your small slam in hearts. When it
holds the trick, he continues optimistically with ◇ J. You ruff
and lay down ♡ A, on which West discards a spade. Plan the
play.

ANSWERS TO QUIZ

1. You plan to take two trump finesses, but a coup may be
necessary if West turns up with a singleton honour. You should
win the lead in dummy and lead ♡ 2, finessing the 10. Assume
this loses to the queen and West switches to a minor suit. You
win in dummy and run ♡ J.

If West shows out on this card, you will be in the right hand to
proceed towards a trump coup. You cash ♠ K, discarding a
club, and ruff ♠ J. You then play three rounds of diamonds,
and ruff ♠ Q. Finally you play the king and ace of clubs. If all
goes well, the lead will be in dummy and your last two cards will
be ♡ A 9 over East's ♡ K 7.

Your play on this hand is known as a *Grand Coup*, because the cards you ruffed to shorten your trumps were winners.

2. After crossing to dummy and finessing ♡ J, you will hold K 10 x x in trumps to East's Q 9. You will therefore need two more diamond ruffs to shorten your trumps sufficiently. That will require four entries to dummy – one for a trump finesse, two for the diamond ruffs and one to make the plain-suit lead towards the trump tenace.

You have two entries in each black suit and you should use the club entries first since East is more likely to be short in that suit. If you use the spade entries first, East may discard from a doubleton club while you are ruffing the diamonds.

Provided no mishap occurs, you will eventually reach this ending:

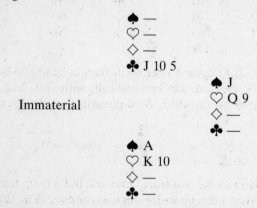

If East discards on ♣ J, you will discard ♠ A and continue with another club to complete the coup.

23

THE UPPERCUT

There are many occasions when an extra trick can be established by encouraging partner to ruff, even when you know that declarer will overruff. Take the East cards here:

```
                    ♠ 8 6 5
                    ♡ 9 8 4 2
                    ◇ K 3
                    ♣ A J 10 4
    ♠ A K J 9 7 2              ♠ Q 3
    ♡ J 3                      ♡ Q 6
    ◇ 10 6 5                   ◇ J 8 7 4 2
    ♣ 5 2                      ♣ K 9 6 3
                    ♠ 10 4
                    ♡ A K 10 7 5
                    ◇ A Q 9
                    ♣ Q 8 7
```

South	West	North	East
1 ♡	1 ♠	2 ♡	No
3 ♣	No	4 ♡	End

Your partner cashes ♠ A K and continues with ♠ J. What will your reaction be? To throw ♣ 9 to let partner know you have the club king? Let's hope not. You must ruff partner's ♠ J with ♡ Q! This will blast a hole in declarer's trump holding, promoting your partner's ♡ J. Later you will score a club trick to put the contract one down. This vicious attack on declarer's trump suit has been aptly named the *Uppercut*. Note how important it was to ruff with your highest trump.

Sometimes more preparation is required. See if you can find the winning defence on the West cards here:

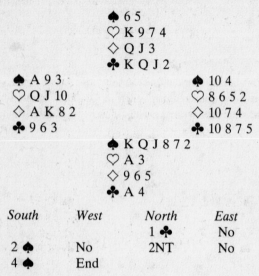

```
                    ♠ 6 5
                    ♡ K 9 7 4
                    ◇ Q J 3
                    ♣ K Q J 2
   ♠ A 9 3                        ♠ 10 4
   ♡ Q J 10                       ♡ 8 6 5 2
   ◇ A K 8 2                      ◇ 10 7 4
   ♣ 9 6 3                        ♣ 10 8 7 5
                    ♠ K Q J 8 7 2
                    ♡ A 3
                    ◇ 9 6 5
                    ♣ A 4
```

South	West	North	East
		1 ♣	No
2 ♠	No	2NT	No
4 ♠	End		

No, we wouldn't open on the North cards either, but you know what some players are like. You lead ◇ A and partner signals with the 4, showing an odd number of diamonds. Declarer is surely marked with the two missing aces, so it seems that the setting trick will have to come from the trump suit. You play two more rounds of diamonds, declarer winning in the dummy.

When a trump is played to the king, you win with the ace and play your thirteenth diamond. Partner knows what is expected of him. He ruffs with ♠ 10, sending declarer's jack flying. Your ♠ 9 is promoted and becomes the setting trick.

With the appalling collection dealt to East on the next hand it would be easy for him to drift off to sleep, hoping for better luck around the corner. Fortunately for his side, West found a way to keep his partner awake.

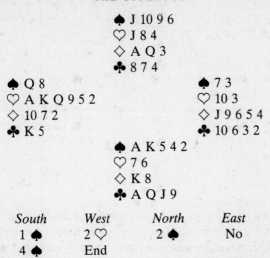

♠ J 10 9 6
♡ J 8 4
◇ A Q 3
♣ 8 7 4

♠ Q 8   ♠ 7 3
♡ A K Q 9 5 2   ♡ 10 3
◇ 10 7 2   ◇ J 9 6 5 4
♣ K 5   ♣ 10 6 3 2

♠ A K 5 4 2
♡ 7 6
◇ K 8
♣ A Q J 9

South	West	North	East
1 ♠	2 ♡	2 ♠	No
4 ♠	End		

West cashed ♡ A K and saw that if partner held as little as ♠ 7 an uppercut would promote a trump trick. To warn partner that he should ruff, West led ♡ 2 at trick 3 rather than ♡ Q.

East realized he had nothing to lose by ruffing with his higher trump and was delighted to see such a modest card force declarer's ♠ K. Declarer played the ace of trumps, finding that he now had a trump loser. Unwilling to rely solely on the club finesse, he eliminated the diamond suit and exited with a trump to West's queen. West was on lead in this end position:

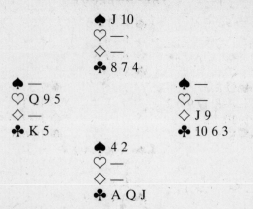

    West had a count of declarer's hand and saw that he would still make a club trick even if he gave declarer a ruff-and-discard. He therefore sealed declarer's fate by exiting in hearts.

    Sometimes declarer can counter an uppercut by discarding a loser at the critical moment. To prevent this, the defenders must be careful to cash any side winners before attempting the promotion.

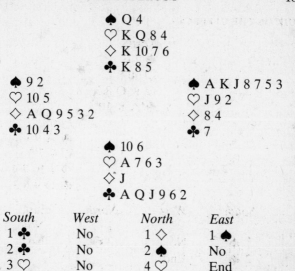

♠ Q 4
♡ K Q 8 4
◇ K 10 7 6
♣ K 8 5

♠ 9 2
♡ 10 5
◇ A Q 9 5 3 2
♣ 10 4 3

♠ A K J 8 7 5 3
♡ J 9 2
◇ 8 4
♣ 7

♠ 10 6
♡ A 7 6 3
◇ J
♣ A Q J 9 6 2

South	West	North	East
1 ♣	No	1 ◇	1 ♠
2 ♣	No	2 ♠	No
3 ♡	No	4 ♡	End

The ♠ 9 is led and East wins with the jack. If he continues with ace and another spade his partner will uppercut with the 10, promoting a trump trick for the defence. It will be in vain, though. Declarer will discard his losing diamond when the third spade is led.

The winning defence is for East to switch to ◇ 8 at trick 2. West wins with the ace and plays a second spade. The third round of spades will now establish the setting trick.

You may wonder why West should continue with spades when in with ◇ A, rather than try to give his partner a diamond ruff. Can you see the clue available to him? If East did have a singleton diamond, he would help his partner find the correct defence by winning the first spade trick with the ace.

QUIZ ON THE UPPERCUT

1.   *North*
                           ♠ 7 6
                           ♡ 10 8 2
                           ◇ K Q 8 3
                           ♣ A K 10 4

                                        East
                                        ♠ A 9
                                        ♡ 9 7 3
                                        ◇ J 10 7 4
                                        ♣ Q 9 6 3

South	*West*	*North*	*East*
		1 ◇	No
1 ♠	No	2 ♣	No
2 ♠	End		

Your partner cashes ♡ A K Q and ◇ A. He then plays a
fourth round of hearts, dummy discarding a diamond. Plan the
defence.

2.   *West*   *East*
               ♠ A K 10 8 6   ♠ 9 7 5 4 2
               ♡ 8 7   ♡ Q J 2
               ◇ A K 5 4   ◇ J 3
               ♣ 10 2   ♣ A Q 4

South	*West*	*North*	*East*
	1 ♠	No	4 ♠
End			

Now you're on the receiving end of an uppercut. North
cashes ♡ A K and continues in mean fashion with a third
round, South ruffing with ♠ Q. Plan the play.

ANSWERS TO QUIZ

1. You must ruff the fourth round of hearts with the ace. This will promote a second trump trick for the defence if partner has as little as ♠ J x x. Remember, you must always ruff high when going for a promotion.

2. If you overruff at trick 3 and find that North started with ♠ J x, the contract will fail when ♣ K is offside. Instead of overruffing the third heart you should discard your potential club loser. You can then win the return, draw trumps and claim the remainder.

24

THE SCISSORS COUP

When you are desperate to keep one particular defender off lead, a loser-on-loser play known as the Scissors Coup may come to your rescue. See how it works here:

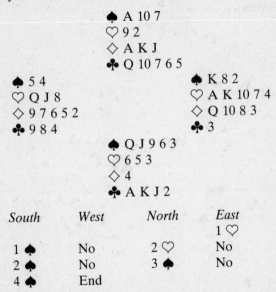

	♠ A 10 7	
	♡ 9 2	
	◇ A K J	
	♣ Q 10 7 6 5	

♠ 5 4		♠ K 8 2
♡ Q J 8		♡ A K 10 7 4
◇ 9 7 6 5 2		◇ Q 10 8 3
♣ 9 8 4		♣ 3

	♠ Q J 9 6 3	
	♡ 6 5 3	
	◇ 4	
	♣ A K J 2	

South	*West*	*North*	*East*
			1 ♡
1 ♠	No	2 ♡	No
2 ♠	No	3 ♠	No
4 ♠	End		

West leads ♡ Q against four spades. East overtakes with ♡ K and returns his singleton club, which you win in hand. If you play on trumps immediately, your fate is clear. East will cross to his partner's ♡ J for a club ruff. One down.

Instead, you must try to cut the link to West's hand. Play three rounds of diamonds, discarding two hearts from hand.

East wins the third round with $\diamond$ Q but has no route to his partner's hand. You will lose only a spade, a heart and a diamond, making the game exactly. By exchanging a heart loser for a diamond loser, you rob the defenders of their club ruff.

On the next hand the defenders threaten a trump promotion. You can put a stop to this with a Scissors Coup.

N–S game

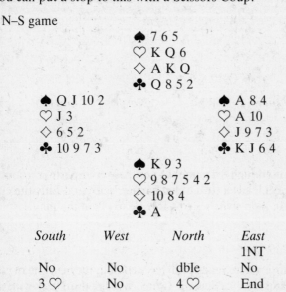

```
              ♠ 7 6 5
              ♡ K Q 6
              ♢ A K Q
              ♣ Q 8 5 2
♠ Q J 10 2                ♠ A 8 4
♡ J 3                     ♡ A 10
♢ 6 5 2                   ♢ J 9 7 3
♣ 10 9 7 3                ♣ K J 6 4
              ♠ K 9 3
              ♡ 9 8 7 5 4 2
              ♢ 10 8 4
              ♣ A
```

South	West	North	East
			1NT
No	No	dble	No
3 ♡	No	4 ♡	End

West leads ♠ Q to his partner's ace. East returns ♠ 8 and you win with the king. You will need to find a 2–2 trump break, but the contract may still fail, even then. If you play on trumps immediately, East will play a third spade to his partner. A fourth round of the suit will then produce an extra trump trick for the defenders.

To prevent this, you must cash ♣ A and cross in diamonds to lead ♣ Q. East has to cover with the king and you dispose of your last spade. By exchanging a spade loser for a club loser, you prevent the defenders crossing for a trump promotion.

You might have made the game another way – by holding off

♠ K until the third round. Since the bidding marked East with
♣ K, the Scissors Coup was a sounder line of play.

QUIZ ON THE SCISSORS COUP
   E – W 30 below

	West		East
	♠ K J 10 8 3		♠ Q 9 7 2
	♡ J 8		♡ A 6
	◇ 9		◇ A Q 8 3
	♣ Q 10 8 6 4		♣ K J 5

South	West	North	East
			1 ◇
No	1 ♠	No	3 ♠
No	No	No	

Three is enough for game, so you pass your partner's double
raise. North leads a club to his partner's ace and ruffs the club
return. He then switches to a low heart. Plan the play.

ANSWER TO QUIZ

As the more astute reader will have sensed, the best line of play
on this hand is . . . a Scissors Coup. Win the third trick with the
ace of hearts and play the ace and queen of diamonds, throwing
a heart from hand if South doesn't cover. This will prevent
South gaining the lead for a possible second club ruff.

If South does cover with ◇ K, you will just have to ruff and
play a trump. The fate of the contract will be out of your hands.

25

THE SIMPLE SQUEEZE (1)

Many players have a mental block about squeeze play, believing it is far too difficult for them to master. Some experts tend to promote this view by writing overlong articles on end positions too abstruse to be of any practical importance. In truth, the most common form of squeeze – the simple squeeze – is quite an elementary technique. Any reader who is still with us at this point in the book will find it easy to grasp.

Let's start by looking at a typical simple squeeze:

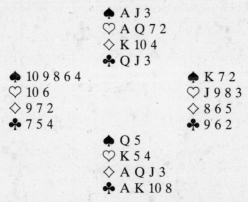

South plays in 7NT and West leads ♠ 10. Since it is inconceivable that West would underlead a king against a grand slam, declarer rises with dummy's ace. There are twelve tricks on top. If declarer simply cashes the three top hearts, he will be disappointed. The suit fails to break 3–3 and the slam goes one down. Instead he should play off all his side-suit winners, moving towards this end position:

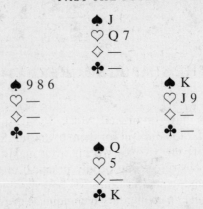

When declarer leads ♣ K, throwing ♠ J from dummy, East is squeezed. Whichever card he throws, he will give declarer an extra trick. He cannot hold in one hand the same number of cards that declarer can in two.

The typical end position we saw had three vital constituents:

(1) The *squeeze card* (♣ K) – the card on which the defender has to discard.

(2) A *one-card menace* (♠ Q) – a threat card guarded by the defender.

(3) A *two-card menace* (♡ Q 7) – a threat card accompanied by a winner.

Except for a few rare positions, all simple squeezes require these three constituents. The squeeze is effective when the two threat cards both lie against the same opponent.

Try a squeeze for yourself now. See if you can spot the squeeze card, the one-card menace and the two-card menace.

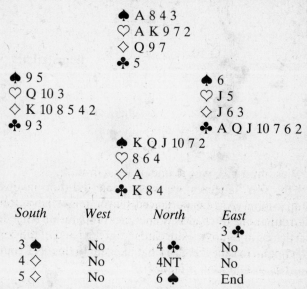

	♠ A 8 4 3	
	♡ A K 9 7 2	
	◇ Q 9 7	
	♣ 5	

♠ 9 5		♠ 6
♡ Q 10 3		♡ J 5
◇ K 10 8 5 4 2		◇ J 6 3
♣ 9 3		♣ A Q J 10 7 6 2

	♠ K Q J 10 7 2	
	♡ 8 6 4	
	◇ A	
	♣ K 8 4	

South	West	North	East
			3 ♣
3 ♠	No	4 ♣	No
4 ◇	No	4NT	No
5 ◇	No	6 ♠	End

West leads ♣ 9 to the ace and East returns ◇ 3. You can count six trump tricks, four side-suit winners and one club ruff. That's eleven. Your twelfth trick will come from a simple squeeze if West holds the heart length and ◇ K.

What will your squeeze card be? The last trump. After you have taken your club ruff, you will run the trump suit. The last trump will squeeze West.

What is your one-card menace? The ◇ Q.

What is your two-card menace? Dummy's ♡ K 9, threatening West's ♡ Q 10.

This will be the end position when you lead your last trump from hand:

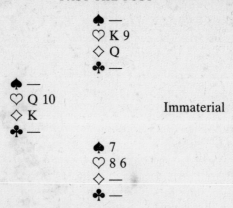

Immaterial

West must give way in one of the red suits.

The two squeezes we have seen did not involve any preparation. An inexperienced player might have stumbled into either one by chance. Sometimes preparation is needed – in particular to remove spare cards from the hand of the defender you intend to squeeze. See what happens in this 6NT contract if no such preparation is made.

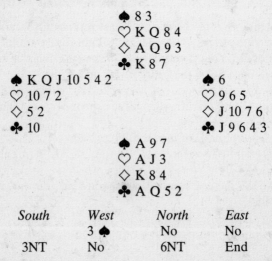

South	West	North	East
	3 ♠	No	No
3NT	No	6NT	End

West leads ♠ K against 6NT. Let's assume you take ♠ A immediately. You have eleven top tricks and a 3–3 break in either minor would provide a twelfth trick. On the bidding, though, it is quite likely that East holds guards in both the minors. In that case perhaps he can be squeezed out of one of his guards.

You test the diamonds, but West discards on the third round. Next you cash two top clubs, West discarding again, and run the heart suit. This is the end position when you lead the last heart from dummy:

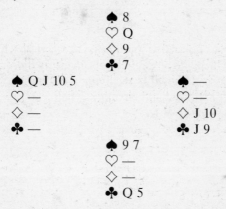

The squeeze card is ♡ Q. The single menace is ♢ 9 and the double menace is ♣ Q 5. But East is not embarrassed by the squeeze card. He simply discards ♢ 10, retaining a guard in both minor suits.

What went wrong? Why did East have a spare card at the end? Because the position was not *tight*. Since the contract was 6NT, one trick was going to be lost anyway. You should have given up that trick early in the play in order to tighten the end position. If you had ducked the opening lead, it would have made a vital difference to the end position. When the squeeze card was led, East would have had one card fewer. This would be the ending:

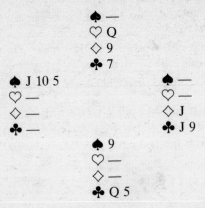

Now East has no card to spare when ♡ Q is led. This process of tightening the hand by deliberately giving up those tricks that you plan to lose is known as *rectifying the count*.

Bear the previous hand in mind when you try this 3NT contract. West leads ♠ K.

```
              ♠ 10 9 6
              ♡ A Q 2
              ◇ K Q 9 4
              ♣ 10 7 2
  ♠ K Q J 8              ♠ 5 3
  ♡ 10 9                 ♡ J 6 5 3
  ◇ 8 5 3                ◇ J 10 7 2
  ♣ Q J 9 4              ♣ K 6 5
              ♠ A 7 4 2
              ♡ K 8 7 4
              ◇ A 6
              ♣ A 8 3
```

You have eight top tricks. Spades are unlikely to divide 3–3, so your best chance of a ninth trick rests with a 3–3 heart break or a simple squeeze in the red suits.

Since your target is nine tricks, you will need to lose four tricks before the squeeze can operate. Duck ♠ K. West continues with ♠ Q, which you duck also. You win the third round of spades and return a spade. You have now lost three of the four tricks you plan to give up. See the effect already on the poor East player! To retain his red-suit guards he has had to discard two clubs. You have more torment in store for him.

West switches to ♡ 10, which you win in the dummy. Now you play a club, ducking when East's king appears. You have now rectified the count. Four tricks have been lost.

East returns a heart, won in the dummy. The hearts fail to break 3–3, but this is the end position when you lead ♣ A:

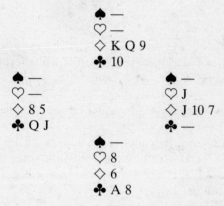

Thanks to your foresight in giving up four tricks early in the play, East now has no spare cards. He must surrender his guard in one of the red suits.

Sometimes giving up a trick will serve a dual purpose. It will rectify the count while at the same time establishing a menace card. Try this 6NT contract:

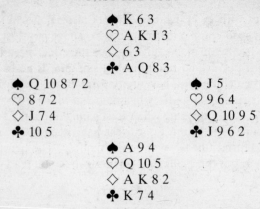

West leads ♡ 8 against 6NT. You have eleven top tricks and a 3–3 club break would give you a twelfth. Isn't there also a chance of a squeeze if the same hand holds four clubs and four diamonds? Yes, there must be. Duck a diamond immediately. This rectifies the count – giving up the one trick that you plan to lose. It also establishes your fourth diamond as a one-card menace; only one defender can hold a guard against it. If the same defender holds club length, you will be able to squeeze him.

Win the defender's return and run your winners. This will be the end position:

The spade ace squeezes East in the minor suits.

QUIZ ON THE SIMPLE SQUEEZE (1)

1.
                    North
                    ♠ J 5 4
                    ♡ K 8 2
                    ♢ A 9 6
                    ♣ A Q 8 7

♢ 10 led

                    South
                    ♠ A K 8 3
                    ♡ A Q 10
                    ♢ K Q 4
                    ♣ K 5 2

South	West	North	East
2NT	No	6NT	End

West leads ♢ 10 against 6NT. Plan the play.

2.
                    North
                    ♠ 9 7
                    ♡ A 3
                    ♢ 8 6 5
                    ♣ A 10 8 6 5 2

♠ K led

                    South
                    ♠ A 8
                    ♡ K Q J 10 9
                    ♢ A K J 4
                    ♣ K 4

South	West	North	East
	3 ♠	No	No
dble	No	5 ♣	No
6 ♡	End		

West leads ♠ K against six hearts.
(a) Plan the play.
(b) What end position do you envisage?

1. You have eleven top tricks and the chance of an immediate twelfth in the spade suit. Win the club lead, cash ♠ A and lead towards ♠ J. If this loses to the queen, you will need one of the black suits to break 3–3 or a black-suit squeeze. Cash your winners in the red suits to arrive at this ending:

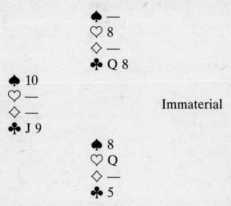

If either defender holds two clubs and the master spade at this stage, he will be squeezed when you play ♡ Q.

2. You will need the diamond finesse to bring your total to eleven tricks. The twelfth might come from a 3–3 diamond break or a minor-suit squeeze on East.

Win the spade lead and return a spade immediately to rectify the count. (This is slightly safer than ducking the opening lead since West might have an eight-card suit.) Win West's return and cross to ♡ A for a diamond finesse. If this succeeds, run the trump suit to arrive at this ending:

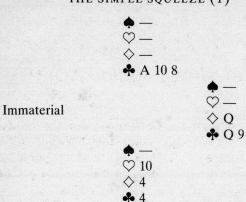

♠ —
♡ —
◇ —
♣ A 10 8

Immaterial

♠ —
♡ —
◇ Q
♣ Q 9

♠ —
♡ 10
◇ 4
♣ 4

If East holds both minor-suit guards at this stage, he will be squeezed when you lead ♡ 10.

In this chapter we will see a few more 'tricks of the trade' used when preparing for a squeeze. One point we did not address in the previous chapter was whether a particular squeeze would work against just one opponent or against either. Look at this end position:

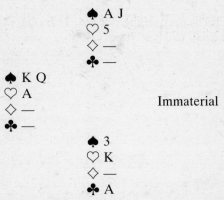

The ♣ A squeezes West in the major suits. If East, instead of West, had held the major-suit guards, the squeeze would still succeed. Such a squeeze, one that works against either opponent, is known as an *automatic squeeze*. It occurs most commonly when the one-card menace lies in the same hand as the squeeze card.

See what happens when the one-card menace is moved to the hand opposite the squeeze card:

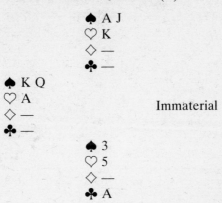

The squeeze still works against West but it would fail if East
held the two guards. Dummy would then have to find a discard
before East. A squeeze that will operate against only one
opponent is known as a *one-way squeeze*.

The Vienna Coup

Let's move to a whole hand now. Can you spot the squeeze
ending here? West leads ♦ 4 against seven diamonds.

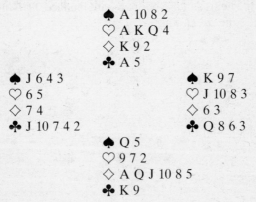

You could draw trumps, test the hearts and arrive at this
ending:

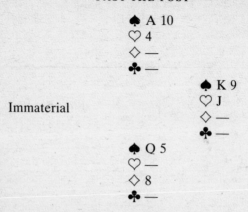

This is a one-way squeeze ending. It will work if West holds the major-suit guards – he will have to discard before the dummy. It fails when, as here, East holds the two guards. If you throw ♠ 10 from dummy, East will throw a spade also. Your ♠ Q is established but you cannot reach it.

To make the contract, whichever defender guards the majors, requires a smart move early in the play. You must cash ♠ A. This frees the ♠ Q to act as a one-card menace. You can then use the heart suit as your two-card menace, arriving at this automatic squeeze ending:

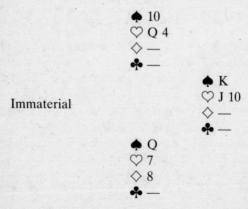

When the squeeze card ($\diamondsuit$ 8) is led, you can spare
♠ 10 from dummy. The defender in the East seat is not so
fortunate. This manoeuvre of unblocking a high card to free a
lesser card as a menace is known as the Vienna Coup. It was the
party piece of a learned Austrian gentleman in the days of
whist.

Isolating the guard

In a trump contract you can sometimes remove one defender's
guard on a side suit by taking one or two ruffs in the suit. The
other defender will be left in sole charge of the suit, rendering
him liable to a squeeze. See how the play develops on this hand.

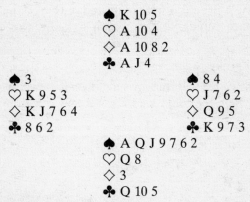

West leads ♣ 2 against six spades. Hoping for the best, you
play low from dummy but East wins with the king and returns
another club. Can you see any chance of making the contract?

You can set up a one-way squeeze on West if he holds $\heartsuit$ K
and at least five diamonds. Draw trumps and ruff a diamond.
Cross to dummy's remaining club honour and ruff another
diamond, removing East's guard in the suit. This will be the end
position when you lead your last trump:

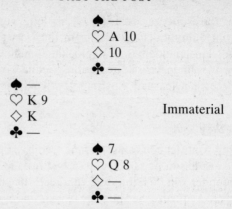

♠ —
♡ A 10
♢ 10
♣ —

♠ —
♡ K 9
♢ K
♣ —

       Immaterial

♠ 7
♡ Q 8
♢ —
♣ —

West must give way in one of the red suits. Your manoeuvre in diamonds – ruffing out East's guard – is known as *isolating the guard*.

Transferring the menace

When it seems that the existing menaces will not prove effective, here is a conjuring trick that may come to your aid:

♠ 9 6 4
♡ A K Q 2
♢ A K 8 2
♣ Q 10

♠ 8 3
♡ J 4
♢ 10 9 6 4 3
♣ J 7 5 4

♠ A K J 10 5
♡ 8 3
♢ J 7
♣ K 9 6 2

♠ Q 7 2
♡ 10 9 7 6 5
♢ Q 5
♣ A 8 3

South	West	North	East
			1 ♠
No	No	dble	No
2 ♡	No	3 ♡	No
4 ♡	End		

You reach four hearts and West leads ♠ 8. East takes two spade tricks and gives his partner a ruff. West exits with a trump and you must somehow take all the remaining tricks.

If West held ♣ K and at least four diamonds, you could catch him in a one-way squeeze. Unfortunately the opening bid makes it a near certainty that East holds ♣ K. There is a fair chance, though, that West holds ♣ J. Draw trumps and lead ♣ Q from dummy. East must cover and you win with the ace. Look what has happened. You have transferred one menace (♣ Q) into another (♣ 10). Now it is West who guards the club suit. Run the trumps and you will arrive at this end position:

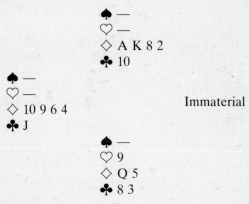

When you lead ♡ 9, West is caught in a one-way squeeze.

QUIZ ON THE SIMPLE SQUEEZE (2)

1.

                         North
                         ♠ A K 2
                         ♡ K 9 8 3
                         ◇ 9 6 5
                         ♣ K 10 4
          ◇ Q led

                         South
                         ♠ J 8 3
                         ♡ A Q 4
                         ◇ A 4
                         ♣ A Q J 9 3

South	*West*	*North*	*East*
		1NT	No
3 ♣	No	3 ♡	No
3NT	No	4 ♣	No
4 ◇	No	4 ♠	No
6 ♣	End		

West leads ◇ Q against six clubs. Plan the play.

2.

North
♠ Q J 5
♡ A Q 7 2
◇ K 8
♣ A 7 5 2

◇ J led

South
♠ A K 10 9 6
♡ 8 5
◇ A 4
♣ K Q 8 6

South	West	North	East
		1NT	No
3 ♠	No	4 ♣	No
4 ◇	No	4 ♡	No
6 ♠	End		

You arrive in a sound spade slam and West leads ◇ J. Plan the play.

ANSWERS TO QUIZ

1. Duck the opening lead to rectify the count. Win the continuation, draw trumps and cash ♠ A K (Vienna Coup) to free your ♠ J as a one-card menace. This will be the ending when you lead your last trump:

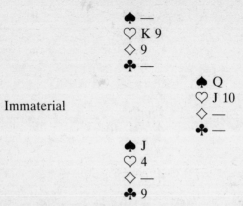

♠ —
♡ K 9
♢ 9
♣ —

Immaterial

♠ Q
♡ J 10
♢ —
♣ —

♠ J
♡ 4
♢ —
♣ 9

If either defender holds ♠ Q and a heart guard (we give the cards to East in the diagram), he will be squeezed when you lead ♣ 9. You will succeed also if West started with six diamonds and four hearts. He will be squeezed in the red suits.

2. Six spades is in danger only when ♡ K is offside and the clubs break 4–1. Win the diamond lead in dummy, draw trumps and take the heart finesse. If this loses, win the return and cross to ♡ A. Now ruff a heart to isolate the heart guard. When you run the trump suit this may be the end position:

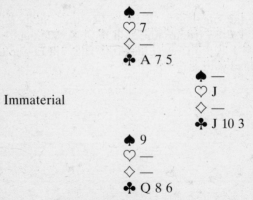

♠ —
♡ 7
♢ —
♣ A 7 5

♠ —
♡ J
♢ —
♣ J 10 3

Immaterial

♠ 9
♡ —
♢ —
♣ Q 8 6

On ♠ 9 you throw a club from dummy. If either defender started with four hearts and four clubs (East, in the diagram), he will be squeezed.

OTHER TYPES OF SQUEEZE

Once the mechanics of the simple squeeze are understood, various other forms of squeeze become easier to grasp. Most important of these is the *double squeeze*, in which both opponents are subjected to a simple squeeze. Here is a typical example:

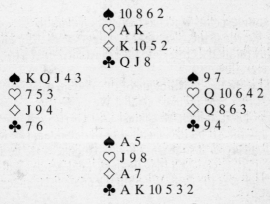

```
              ♠ 10 8 6 2
              ♡ A K
              ◇ K 10 5 2
              ♣ Q J 8
♠ K Q J 4 3                    ♠ 9 7
♡ 7 5 3                        ♡ Q 10 6 4 2
◇ J 9 4                        ◇ Q 8 6 3
♣ 7 6                          ♣ 9 4
              ♠ A 5
              ♡ J 9 8
              ◇ A 7
              ♣ A K 10 5 3 2
```

West leads ♠ K against 6NT. There are eleven top tricks and it is a natural move for you to duck the first trick to rectify the count. You win the spade continuation, unblock the hearts and run the club suit. This classical ending results:

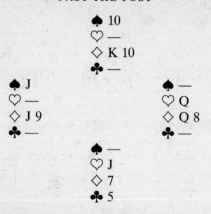

♠ 10
♡ —
♢ K 10
♣ —

♠ J
♡ —
♢ J 9
♣ —

♠ —
♡ Q
♢ Q 8
♣ —

♠ —
♡ J
♢ 7
♣ 5

On your last club West has to abandon diamonds to retain his spade guard. You dispose of dummy's ♠ 10, which has manfully fulfilled its role, and East must surrender a trick in one of the red suits.

What were the constituents of this double squeeze?

(a) A one-card menace against West (♠ 10);

(b) a one-card menace against East (♡ J); and

(c) a two-card menace against both defenders (♢ K 10).

With this type of squeeze, one-card menaces are more likely to prove effective when they lie over the defender who guards them. That was the case with both the one-card menaces on the hand above.

Try a double squeeze for yourself now. Look for two one-card menaces and a two-card menace that exerts pressure against both defenders.

South	West	North	East
South	*West*	*North*	*East*
3 ♣	No	5 ♣	End

West leads ♠ A and you regret your enterprising opening bid when the dummy appears. Still, if things do go wrong, at least you will be able to blame partner for not finding the 'obvious' 3NT bid.

West cashes a second high spade and switches to ◇ 2. Since West had several safe exits available, you are inclined to place ◇ Q with East. It is likely also that ♡ K is with West, as otherwise a heart switch would have been more natural. If the cards lie as you imagine, a double squeeze is already coming into focus. West will have to guard the spades; East will have to guard the diamonds. Neither will be able to guard the third round of hearts.

Is any preparation required? Yes, you will have to ruff a spade to isolate the guard with West. You will also have to cash ◇ A K (Vienna Coup) to free ◇ J as a one-card menace against East. This will be the ending:

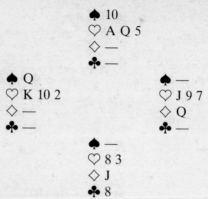

Each defender in turn will have to throw a heart on your last trump. You will score three heart tricks. No need to criticize partner's bidding now, of course. It would distract everyone from praising your card-play.

One of the prettiest plays in the game is the *criss-cross squeeze*. This occurs when at least one of the menaces is blocked, in a situation such as singleton ace opposite Q x. Watch the ending develop on this hand:

```
                    ♠ Q 7 2
                    ♡ A K 4
                    ♢ Q 8 3 2
                    ♣ J 10 5
   ♠ 10                            ♠ 8 6 4
   ♡ 8 6 3 2                       ♡ Q J 9
   ♢ J 9 7 6 5                     ♢ K 10 4
   ♣ 9 8 6                         ♣ A K Q 3
                    ♠ A K J 9 5 3
                    ♡ 10 7 5
                    ♢ A
                    ♣ 7 4 2
```

South	West	North	East
			1 ♣
1 ♠	No	2 ♣	No
3 ♠	No	4 ♠	End

West leads ♣ 9 against four spades. East cashes three rounds of the suit and switches to ♡ Q. It seems likely that East holds ◇ K and ♡ J, but how can you squeeze him? There doesn't seem to be a two-card menace. Run the trump suit and see what happens:

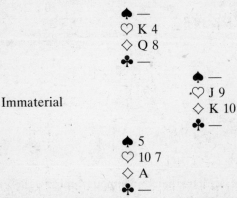

```
              ♠ —
              ♡ K 4
              ◇ Q 8
              ♣ —
                          ♠ —
                          ♡ J 9
   Immaterial             ◇ K 10
                          ♣ —
              ♠ 5
              ♡ 10 7
              ◇ A
              ♣ —
```

On your last spade you throw ♡ 4 from dummy, leaving both your menaces blocked. East must now abandon one of the red suits. Provided you can read which suit is unguarded (East may try to fool you by unguarding a suit early in the play), you will be able to untangle your tricks.

A closely related play is the trump squeeze, where you threaten to establish an extra trick by ruffing. Here is a straightforward example:

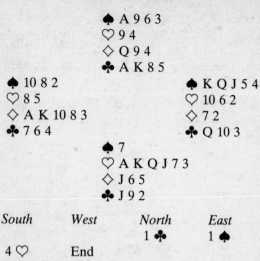

South	West	North	East
		1 ♣	1 ♠
4 ♡	End		

West begins with his diamond honours and gives his partner a ruff. The spade king is returned. What now? Isolating the spade guard and running the trump suit will not bring any joy; North will be squeezed in front of East. Instead, take just one spade ruff before running the trumps. This will be the ending:

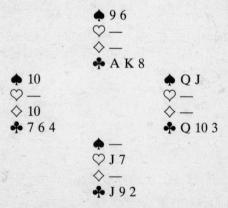

On your penultimate trump you throw ♣ 8 from dummy and East is already squeezed. If he throws a spade you can establish a spade trick in dummy. If he unguards the club queen you can cash ♣ A K and return to hand with a ruff to enjoy ♣ J. Note that for a trump squeeze to work you need two entries to the hand opposite the squeeze card; in this case, the ace and king of clubs.

To admire such intricacies as the *triple repeating guard squeeze with double-delayed duck*, you will need a tome more learned than this one. And the best of luck to you!

QUIZ ON OTHER TYPES OF SQUEEZE

1.

North
♠ 8
♡ A K 8
♢ A 8 7 2
♣ A K 10 7 2

♢ Q led

South
♠ A K Q J 10 6
♡ 7 3
♢ K 5
♣ 8 6 3

South	West	North	East
1 ♠	No	3 ♣	No
4 ♠	No	7 ♠	End

You show your solid spade suit and partner takes a flyer at the grand slam. West leads ♢ Q. Plan the play.

2.

North
♠ J 8 6 3
♡ A 9 6 4
◇ A 10
♣ 10 8 2

♠ 10 led

South
♠ 2
♡ Q 5
◇ K Q
♣ A K Q J 9 7 6 5

South	West	North	East
		No	4 ♠
5 ♣	No	6 ♣	End

Showing due respect for your dummy play, partner raises you to six clubs. West leads ♠ 10, which you cover in dummy. East wins with the ace and returns another high spade. How will you justify partner's faith in you?

ANSWERS TO QUIZ

1. West's lead, doubtless from a sequence, makes it quite likely that he holds the diamond length. If East has at least three clubs there will be a double squeeze. Win the lead in hand, draw trumps and cash ♣ A K (Vienna Coup). Then play ◇ A and ruff a diamond to isolate the diamond guard with West. If the cards lie as you hope, this will be the ending:

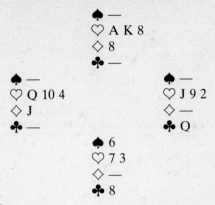

On your last trump each defender in turn will have to abandon the heart suit.

2. If East holds ♡ K, you can catch him in a trump squeeze. Ruff the second spade high and run the trump suit. This will be the ending:

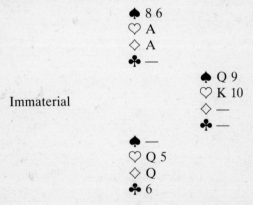

When you cross to ◇ A, East will be squeezed. Since you have a count on the spade suit, he will not even be able to put you to a guess.